Victoria Marmot
and the
Road to Hell

Virginia McClain

Front cover design by Natasha Snow
Back cover and spine by Virginia McClain

Works by Virginia McClain

The Victoria Marmot series:
Victoria Marmot and the Meddling Goddess
Victoria Marmot and the Inconvenient Prophecy
Victoria Marmot and the Shadow of Death
Victoria Marmot and the Dragon's Rage
Victoria Marmot and the Road to Hell
Victoria Marmot: The Complete Collection (Books 1 - 5)

The Chronicles of Gensokai series:
Blade's Edge
Traitor's Hope

Short Stories
*Rain on a Summer's Afternoon**

To Dad, for always having a sense of humor.

THE NOTHINGNESS WAS absolutely terrifying.

I would probably have shit my pants,
except I didn't appear to have any
pants, let alone an intestinal tract with which to
shit them. In fact, even the sensation of terror felt
slightly off, because I had no heart to race, no pulse
to quicken, no breath to catch.

An instant ago, I had been surrounded by friends
in a world I recognized. Then Trev had admitted
he'd known about Mom and Dad being alive, I'd
freaked out, reached through time and space while
only wanting to disappear, and now…

I had nothing.

I could see nothing. No light, no shadow, no hint
of shapes in darkness, just… nothing.

Even that would have been manageable, I think, if I could have felt anything. Anything at all. But for a moment, for as long as it took me to register that I didn't seem to have a body, or anything at all to contain me—whatever qualified as "me" in that instant—I was nothing.

Nothing but thoughts.

And then, as suddenly as the thought occurred to me—in the instant in which my mind wanted my body to be there—it was. I still couldn't see it, or anything else, but I could feel my hands, feet, heart beating, lungs breathing, all the little twitches and ticks that make up a body.

And the moment that I longed to see that body, if only to confirm that I wasn't somehow hallucinating it, I could.

There was light, though it was the strangest light I'd ever experienced, since it seemed to have no origin, and lit nothing but my body. There was no source, and my body cast no shadows. The light wasn't coming from within me, but a glow surrounded me like a tightly wrapped blanket.

It was just enough to confirm that I had eyes to see and a body to feel. A naked one, for a heartbeat anyway, until I thought that I'd rather not be, and was suddenly covered in some galaxy leggings and a soft t-shirt with "i^2 (keep it real)" emblazoned on the chest.

"Better than what my Gwen powers keep choosing," I said, into the nothing. Because even though I now had a clothed body that I could feel, there was still nothing around me. So much so, that I wondered how I was speaking aloud. I supposed there must be oxygen, since I was still alive and didn't even feel out of breath, but there was certainly no motion of air around me, or even a sense of what was up or down. I felt as though I were floating in space, only without all the freezing to death, having all your blood vessels burst, and asphyxiation.

Then I wondered if the reason that I wasn't dying was simply because I was already dead.

What else would cause me to be suspended in nothing, as a string of thoughts that seemed to be able to will myself into being?

Beginning to panic, and now with a body that latched fully onto the sensation of a tightening chest and more rapid breathing, I closed my eyes and tried to shift back to the dragon realm. I reached for it with every fiber of my being. Stretched desperately for that field in the sunlight, where I'd just reappeared in front of all of my friends after my crazy trip through hell.

And got nothing but the mother of all headaches in return.

That did not help the rising panic situation.

I tried to take some deep, calming breaths and focus on lowering my heart rate.

To my amazement, it worked.

Although I wasn't sure why I was surprised. If I'd just managed to think galaxy leggings into existence, why not calm my breathing with a thought too? Which sort of just reinforced the idea that none of this was real. Which brought me back to being convinced that I was dead. And…cue chest tightening.

"Damn it! Calm the fuck down, Vic."

And ok, apparently yelling at myself worked too. As soon as I said the words, my heart rate returned to normal again.

I closed my eyes again, and tried reaching for every location I could think of: the glade of Life, Sol's cabin in the Andes, the ruins of my old house in Arizona, the ruins of my older home in Colorado, Uncle Algy's place, Flagstaff High School—nothing worked. I remained surrounded by nothing.

"This is getting kinda old," I informed the nothing.

"I would really prefer it if I had someone to talk to," I added, hopefully.

Since I'd been half expecting to conjure another person out of thin air, I should not have nearly jumped out of my skin when I heard a soft thump to my right. I did anyway.

But when I turned to inspect the blackness there, I didn't see anything.

"I would love to be able to see the someone I can talk to," I clarified, and immediately gasped, finding myself confronted with a very large, very toothy snow leopard.

"**P**LEASE DON'T EAT me."

Of course, right after I said it, the giant snow leopard's jaw snapped shut in the final throes of what, now, was clearly a yawn, but that didn't make my ass unclench, or keep my stomach from feeling like it was doing somersaults for a while. Instead, it blew a huff of air out of its nose and twitched its expansive whiskers, before stepping past me and into... a room that hadn't existed a second ago.

Dark hardwood flooring stretched beneath a throw rug, low coffee table, and some plush leather couches. There was also a fireplace, complete with a crackling fire and the smell of cedar smoke. Given that the place looked and smelled like a cozy combination of my parents' Colorado living room and Sol's Andean cabin, someone was trying to make me feel better.

Belatedly, it occurred to me that someone was probably me.

The excessively large snow leopard waltzed past me, past the coffee table, and onto the dark leather sofa. There, she twitched her large, fluffy tail a few times before pressing her furry head into the sofa cushion and blinking sleepily at me.

It was then, gazing into eyes that weren't the dazzling grey exhibited by most snow leopards, but instead ringed in a bright green like my own, that I realized exactly who I was staring at.

"You're me, aren't you?" I asked, unsure if that was the right way to phrase it. "Or, me when I'm a snow leopard, anyway."

Feline me merely blinked at me again, then shut her eyes and began purring softly.

"Well, fuck. I was kinda hoping for someone to talk *to*, you know. Not just someone to talk *at*."

Snow leopard me said nothing, but the large oak door to the room, which hadn't been there a moment ago, suddenly reverberated with a deep and echoing thump.

"Well, that's not terrifying," I said, reluctantly turning away from snow leopard me and heading towards the newly existent door.

I F STARING DOWN snow leopard me had been disconcerting, staring into the plate-sized eyes of a dragon was as terrifying as the nothingness of death.

"You can turn off the 'make the human shit her pants glamour' any time now," I said, by way of introduction.

"I am not using my glamour, Vic. It's just that dragons are terrifying up close. Even when they're you."

That voice wasn't mine. Or, at least, it didn't come from my human mouth. What qualified as "mine" in this place was getting stupidly more complicated by the second.

"I suppose we're all here?" asked the dragon, poking her head, which was about five times the size of the average horse head, into the room.

"Hey, Kit!" she exclaimed, addressing the still sleeping feline, whose tail flicked in a semi-conscious gesture of welcome.

"Mind making the room bigger, Vic?"

The dragon turned her giant head in my direction again, and I realized she was talking to me. I had been too stunned by her overall appearance to really listen to her. Unlike my snow leopard form, which I had at least seen in the mirror once, I'd never gotten to look at any part of my dragon form for more than a few fleeting seconds while I was inhabiting its skin. Or its scales, I suppose I should say.

"Room, be bigger," I said, not sure how to make things adjust intentionally without voicing my requests, and finding myself too distracted by dragon-me's beauty to even notice how much larger the room and door got. Instead, I stood mesmerized, as dragon-me pushed her enormous, scaled body into a room that was now large enough to encompass her in all of her sunset-colored glory. I'd forgotten just how stunning those scales were. Perhaps not surprising, considering I'd never gotten more than a peripheral glimpse of them. Seeing them full-on, and from the perspective of a human, was completely entrancing. Almost hypnotic.

"I know, we're lovely, aren't we?"

I blinked, distantly noticing that the voice wasn't mine.

"Why have I never noticed that I can speak aloud in dragon form?" I asked, suddenly embarrassed.

"Yes, well, you're rather new to the whole being a dragon thing, aren't you? And I… well, I don't exactly have more experience—I haven't existed any longer than you have, since we're the same person really, but without human thoughts to distract me it all just sort of… works. You'll need practice, of course, but dragon vocal chords are incredibly versatile. There's little we can't do with them. Anyway, I didn't mean to show off, but since you were already speaking aloud with Kit, I thought it was only polite to do the same."

I took a deep breath and decided to focus on the last thing dragon-me had just said.

"You heard me speaking to her?"

"More or less. I was you while you were speaking to her, so I heard everything."

"And you're not me now?" I asked, starting to wish I were sitting down. As soon as the thought formed, I was sitting on a large, dark leather sofa perpendicular to the one where feline-me slept.

"Ok, this place is freaking me out," I admitted.

"Yes, I'd noticed. I suppose that's understandable. You're never conscious when you're here, after all. None of us are, usually."

"Where, exactly, is here?" I asked, trying not to wince.

"Well, that's complicated, but the short answer is… the extradimensional pocket where you keep all your dark matter."

"Isn't my dark matter inside me, spread throughout my blood?"

"Yep."

"So, I'm inside myself?"

"Sort of."

"That doesn't seem like a place I ought to be able to go," I said, feeling my mind trying to bend around to understand dragon-me's explanation.

"It does seem implausible," she agreed. "But here we are."

"How could I possibly have gotten here?"

"I'm guessing it had something to do with your Gwen-given abilities, but I'm not entirely sure, to be honest."

"And if you're me… how do you know anything that I don't already know?"

"Oooh! That's a good one. The answer is that I'm a dragon. Which is to say, you're at least part dragon. And I don't know anything that you don't technically know."

"What?"

Dragon-me stared at human-me and blinked her giant, green eyes.

"You know everything I do, technically, but dragon brains and human brains don't work the same way, so it would be difficult for you to know the things that I know when you aren't in dragon form."

"And how on earth do you know things that I don't know regardless of what form you're in? Were you… did you…" I swallowed, feeling suddenly ill. "Did I steal a dragon when I—"

"No, no. Good heavens no. Nothing like that. I'm a part of you, accessed through your well of dark matter and a bit of epigenetic gymnastics. You didn't steal an already existing dragon, but… dragons, even weredragons, are a bit of an odd case in the grand scheme of things. Dragons have very large brains, and cerebral matter that is unlike that of any other creature's. It grants us a few advantages. For one, we have genetic memory. Very strong genetic memory, unlike most species, so we keep all the knowledge of our species alive even without an oral or written history (though of course we have those as well). Full dragons are born knowing everything that every single one of their ancestors knew. They are born with dozens, or hundreds, of lives in their memories. Were-dragons only get a sort of distilled version of that, since they originally come from a human and dragon pairing up while the dragon is in its human form. But even that little bit of human DNA makes the genetic memory less detailed than a full dragon's memory, since half or more of their ancestors don't have the genetic memory to fill in the blanks. And whatever memories they have, they can only access them when they're in dragon form."

"Holy shit."

"Indeed."

"So… because you're currently in our dragon form, you know that stuff, but I don't?"

"Well, in this space you might actually be able to access my genetic memory without me being in dragon form, but it might be difficult to visualize, and it's hard to look for something you don't know you have. Since you wished for company, and then company that could talk, here we are."

"**M**Y HEAD HURTS, and it's not from trying to shift myself out of here," I muttered.

Dragon-me looked completely nonplussed, inasmuch as I could distinguish facial expressions on her scaled mien, and feline-me let out a low noise that sounded suspiciously like a growl.

"What?" I asked, glancing between the two of them.

"Aren't you concerned about the fact that shifting out of here didn't work?" dragon-me asked.

I didn't like her tone. It was far too cautious. Like she was worried she'd hurt me if she spoke any louder.

"Of course I am. Weren't you there for the near panic attack I had? What's your point?"

I sounded too shrill even to my own ears, but I couldn't help it. Just bringing it up again made me feel jittery.

"It shouldn't be possible for you to be here," dragon-me said, lending an extra calm to her voice that had the opposite effect than she was probably going for. "All three of us being here means there is no part of your consciousness outside of this space, and thus no tether to shift back with."

"Does that mean that all three of us are actually separate parts of my consciousness?" I asked, wondering if what I actually had was a multiple personality disorder.

Feline-me growled at that suggestion.

"Look, as far as I can tell, our situation here is unique," dragon-me offered. "No dragon in our ancestry had a clear understanding of how dark matter pockets worked, because most of our ancestors were more of the "magic is magic" mindset. But even the one draconic scientist whose genetic memory I possess was never able to access her own dark matter pocket, even after she'd theorized that it existed. She actually tried, of course, scientist that she was, but she only managed to bring out her human form or send it away. She never managed to travel to the pocket herself. Which, of course, only cemented her hypothesis."

"Which was?"

"Her hypothesis? That it was impossible to access one's own dimensional pocket. All her research confirmed it."

"Yeah, well, I doubt any of her test subjects had access to Gwen-given powers."

"True. I've never heard of anyone pulling people through time and space the way Gwen does, or the way that you do."

"Yeah, I didn't think that much of it—I mean aside from thinking it was badass—until Torrence started explaining how mages jump through time and space."

I sighed, almost feeling queasy at the memory of how stitching multiple pocket dimensions together had made Sol throw up. Then I sat up abruptly, as an idea came to me.

"What if I tried it the old fashioned mage way?"

Dragon-me blinked a few times.

"I don't know why that would work when the Gwen-given shift doesn't. If anything, it's just more complicated and—"

"I have to at least try," I interrupted.

Dragon-me didn't argue, but the look in her giant reptilian eyes wasn't exactly encouraging.

I closed my eyes, reaching for a nearby pocket dimension, and… and realized I had no idea what pocket dimension paralleled the dragon realm. Or anywhere. Or how I was supposed to reach for a pocket dimension rather than just reaching for the place I was trying to go.

"I believe it takes mages years of practice and study before they can shift through multiple planes," dragon-me explained.

I sighed, my headache returning with a vengeance.

"And I doubt you'd be able to shift away from here that way even if you'd had years of practice. After all, this pocket dimension lies within you. Without a piece of your soul anchoring you to the world, you have no tether to follow. No way to—"

"Wait. What did you say?" I asked.

"I said—"

"Never mind, I know what you said."

I hated to be rude, but my brain had finally caught up with what my ears had processed.

"Anchor, tether, soul," I mumbled.

Then I closed my eyes and searched my soul. I wasn't sure I really believed in a soul, as such. Agnosticism was about as far as my spirituality had ever gone, and I was pretty firmly in the atheism camp these days, but if dark matter had taught me anything, it was that there was more to human life that our current science could fully explain. I didn't doubt that we'd get there with time, but…let's just say, I was more open to ideas that didn't meet with current scientific scrutiny at the moment. So I closed my eyes and tried to visualize what my spirit might look like, if I could see it. At first I pictured a semitransparent version of me, but that just made me think of low-end special effects from the 90s, so I decided to switch tactics. I pictured a glowing green sphere instead, one that matched the color of my eyes in all three of my forms. Didn't someone once say that eyes were windows to the soul? So I went with that. When I pictured the glowing green ball of energy at my core, I searched it for the various tethers I might have to the place I wanted to return. I found three of them. Two were tiny, new, and barely large enough to notice. Some instinct told me they wouldn't help me get anywhere. But the third one was at least a third of the size of the whole ball. It was large, and bright, and I knew exactly who it led to.

I also knew that I wasn't going to be able to use it unless I forgave him. The whole reason I was here was that I'd been so distraught at the idea of my brother keeping secrets from me, namely the secret that our parents were both alive and in touch with him, that I'd felt a need to run away so strong that I hadn't even picked a place to run away to. I'd wound up here instead. The thought still rankled, but I took a few deep breaths and tried to think about things from Trev's perspective. Then I realized that I didn't even know what Trev's perspective was. I hadn't given him a chance to explain. I'd just felt hurt, hopeless, and bitter, then reached into the void. That was hardly Trev's fault. I owed him a chance to explain himself. I owed him enough empathy to try to understand why he hadn't told me our parents were alive. And even if I didn't owe it to him, I didn't want to withhold it. I wanted my twin back. We'd been separated for so damned long, for reasons out of our control, and now I was voluntarily walking away from him, just because he'd done something I didn't understand.

That didn't feel right.

That felt awful.

In that instant, I wanted nothing more than to be by my brother's side.

And then I was.

I LOOKED UP and found myself staring straight into Trevor's eyes. The hurt in them, the fear, made me look down at my own body just to be sure that I was actually in one piece.

I looked reassuringly whole.

"Vic?" asked Trev and Sol, at the same time.

I looked between them, and realized, with more than a little bit of shock, that they were standing exactly where I'd left them. We were all standing in a field full of dragons preparing for war, the grass was thick beneath my feet and the sky shone clear and blue above us. Azrael was still off a ways discussing Gwen knew what with General Aira, and I was standing encircled by all of the people that I'd held most dear. Standing in the exact spot I'd tried to will myself back to a hundred times from that little dimensional pocket. Standing in front of all of the people I'd tried to will myself back to. But the only one I'd been able to reach had been Trev. People said a lot of weird shit about twins and the ties that bind them. I'd always thought some of it was true. After all, Trev and I had spent the past three weeks communicating mind to mind, but…well, maybe more of it was true than I'd thought.

"Well, shit," I said, trying to will my legs to continue to hold me, even though they both felt like poorly formed jello. "How long was I gone?"

Sol, Rhelia, Trev, and Seamus all exchanged glances.

"You did not go anywhere," Rhelia said cautiously.

"It kind of looked like you shifted," Seamus admitted. "But at the end of the shift, it was still you, in human form, albeit in different clothes."

I looked down again and barely registered that I was still wearing galaxy leggings and my nerdiest t-shirt.

"You're saying that no time has passed?" I asked, feeling the same headache that had been plaguing me ever since I got to the dimensional pocket coming on once more. Everyone shook their heads.

"You ssssaid, 'You knew they were there. Thissss whole time. You knew.' And then you ssssort of phassssed in and out, and now you don't look quite well," said Rhelia, in a matter-of-fact tone.

I nodded, thinking that my life was one of the most ridiculous strings of events I'd ever heard of—causing me to wonder briefly if the author of my story actually existed, and if so, if she got paid very well—and then I promptly passed the fuck out.

W HEN I OPENED my eyes next, I was gazing into the bright silver gaze of the most beautiful person I'd ever seen. I had to blink a few times to realize that it was Az.

Their face was close enough that I could feel their breath on my lips, which felt warm and wet— as if they'd just been kissed. I was somewhat startled to find my arms wrapped enthusiastically around Az's neck. "What happened?" I breathed.

Every fiber of me positively buzzed with the need to continue whatever Az had started. My brain felt muddled, but the headache was gone, and my vision was quite a bit sharper than it had been just before I'd passed out. Sharp enough that I could make out the dragon army still marshaling for war around us, along with my friends standing much closer and looking far more concerned than I would have expected.

"You passed out, Luv. I caught you before you planted your face in the mud, and did what I could to transfer you a bit of energy. Didn't want to do too much, since you weren't awake and I like my partners consenting, but I figured you'd prefer it to sleeping for the next three days. Though that's still an option, if you choose not to seal the deal."

Az winked, and I couldn't decide if I wanted to punch them or kiss them again.

I decided instead to just push myself out of their embrace.

"Hang on, Luv, you probably don't have enough—"

Az didn't get to finish whatever they were saying before I'd pushed myself out of their arms and promptly found myself in a heap on the ground.

"Ouch," I muttered.

"I didn't give you much energy. Like I said, I wanted your consent. So I figured if I gave you enough of a boost to wake you up, we could talk, and you'd be in a better state of mind to say whether or not you'd like my help."

I tried to get up off the ground, but found myself completely unable to move. I could twitch, at least. Enough to let me know that I wasn't paralyzed, but it was as if all of my muscles had shorted somehow, and there was no more strength in any part of my body.

"The fastest way to heal you up would be to get completely intimate, but I remember you expressing your doubts about my trustworthiness as a succubus the last time that came up, so I rather thought you'd appreciate a discussion first."

"How does me letting you steal my soul help me, exactly?" I asked, baffled, from my prone spot on the downtrodden muddy grass.

"It's not stealing your soul. Well, it can be, if I'm using myself as a weapon, but a real exchange is precisely that—an exchange. It's give *and* take, and we'd both benefit from it."

I thought of the glowing green ball I'd just discovered while locked in my own dimensional pocket; the idea of siphoning off a portion of that glow to give to Azrael, even in exchange for some super-duper energy boost, did not particularly appeal. I cringed from where I lay, wondering why none of my other friends were coming to my aid.

"This is ridiculous," I muttered. "I'm just going to shift to Life's glade and get him to heal me up."

I closed my eyes and pulled on space and time, barely hearing the cries of "Vic, no!" from around me, as darkness reached up and snatched me from the living.

I REGAINED CONSCIOUSNESS in a darkened room, surrounded with low-burning, spice-scented candles, and some soft orchestral music playing in the background.

Then I heard the shuffling of feathers, and my gaze caught on a set of glinting silver eyes very close to my own.

"Why have I never noticed that your eyes are silver?" I asked, feeling a surge of guilt as well as wonder. Az's eyes were the most startling metallic silver I'd ever seen, and they practically glowed in contrast with their ebon skin. I leaned back, putting a bit more distance between us, and took in Az's hair. It was all white, in a glorious set of braids that fell well past their silver wings, all the way to their waist.

"It's part of my magic, Luv. Difficult to blend into the human population like this, even if I hide my wings. So, I sort of repel the gaze from my eyes, hair, wings, and ears."

"Ears?"

And then it was like my eyes finally registered the entirety of Az's face. Their ears were ever-so-slightly pointed, nothing like the dagger tips of the few elves I'd met, but pointed enough not to pass for human. I stared at Az and realized that, while I'd already considered them to be possibly the most beautiful person I'd ever seen, the eyes, hair, and ears took things to an ethereal level. I wasn't much for biblical literature, but I thought maybe I understood where the concept of angels had come from.

"Why can I see you properly now?" I asked, mesmerized.

"We're alone, and I'm rather interested in having you see me as I really am, at the moment. I'm sorry for kissing you without your consent, but I couldn't get your consent when you were unconscious, and I wanted you awake and alive to either rip me to shreds or accept my proposal. If we weren't about to go to war, I'd never have done even that much without your enthusiastic agreement."

Az stood up then, and as I focused on the rest of their body, my pulse quickened. My body was enthusiastically prepared to consent to anything Az wanted. They were wearing a gorgeous emerald green brocade corset with black edging and some light-absorbing gems studded periodically around the edging. The corset was gorgeous, but it alone wouldn't have stolen my breath away, even coupled with the supple leather pants that hugged tight to Azrael's legs. It was the fact that I could see both of Az's forms, and that they both wore the same outfit—though it was clearly tailored to suit their very different figures. The overlap made me dizzy, as usual, but I closed my eyes and focused my mind for a moment before opening them again.

I'd never seen a man in a corset before.

Az was gorgeous in both forms, and I obviously had a difficult time deciding a preference, as evidenced by how often I saw both of them, but I really wanted a moment to savor the novelty of the male corset before I went back to seeing double, or maybe just enjoying the female aspect. I swallowed, desire pulsing through my body, and then winced when I realized that my body was in an almost overwhelming amount of pain. The fact that I could feel any desire at all in that moment spoke to Az's powers as a succubus.

"You look awful, Luv," Az said, from the spot where they now stood encircled in candlelight. I blinked as my vision shifted and I saw both of them again. Apparently, it took more energy than I had to keep them separate.

"Thanks. Wish I could say the same about you," I wheezed, letting my head fall back against the pillow behind me. That was the first moment I noticed that I was in a bed. I could feel the scarring on my neck, face, and arm pull tight as I tried to lower myself into the mattress, and the reminder of their presence did nothing for my self esteem, but I tried to brush the thought away.

"I thought you wanted my consent," I added, feeling a bit salty about having been placed in a bed surrounded by candles, even as I let my eyes close against the pain.

"I do, Luv. I won't do anything without your permission. Seamus and Sol helped me bring you here, and I only gave you one more kiss, enough to help you regain consciousness, nothing more. I don't want you to do anything you don't want to do, but we've got work to do, and a universe to save, and if you've any interest in being able to help, you need this."

I thought about that for a moment. Az's power scared me, but how much of that was simply that I didn't understand it?

"Are they still launching the attack against MOME?"

Az's expression went from sultry to troubled.

"Yes. I explained everything we'd learned to General Aira, but they aren't planning to hold back against MOME. Albert wants to talk to you—he has a lot of questions, but Seamus and Sol said you were in no condition to answer them, and they were right. You weren't even conscious, and you still wouldn't be right now if I hadn't given you a bit more of my power to help you out. With everything you've gone through, you'd be lucky if you woke up in a week."

I laughed, or would have, but it only came out as a agonized huff.

"You don't know the half of it," I whispered.

"We don't have much time if we're going to try to stop Dryer, Luv. You and I both know that a full strike on MOME isn't going to stop this if she keeps going. We need to go after Dryer herself, and we need to do it before she can go to ground. I know you don't trust my power, but… after all we've been through together, can't you believe that I would never hurt you?"

I raised my head just enough to look Az in the eyes, and realized that what I saw reflected back at me was pain. Damn. That stung. Az had, despite plenty of reasons not to bother, always tried to help me. They'd saved my life more than once, and we'd literally walked through Hell together…

"Tell me how your power works," I said, knowing that information was likely to be the only thing that would calm the fear coiling inside me, even if we didn't really have time for it.

"The short version is that anytime I'm intimate with someone, I have two choices: I can just take, or I can give and take. Oddly enough, I can't just give. I've tried. It never works. I'm a succubus. My power comes from life energy, but specifically in the form of sexual energy. I generate lust in people simply by breathing, generally, and if I siphon that off, it's enough to sustain me, but a succubus becomes more powerful by taking more than lust. It only sticks if I give back, though. I can only make permanent changes to myself or others through a full exchange."

Azrael sighed.

"If it makes you feel any better, I almost never offer a full exchange. I can get by quite nicely just siphoning off a bit of lust here or there, or consummating with a normal human and skimming a bit of their unused energy in the course of events. That's enough to keep me going. A full exchange gives a part of my strength to the receiving party, just as it takes a bit of their strength for myself. It's not something I do lightly."

"Demons are weird," I chuckled, realizing that the fact that Azrael's biology was so incredibly distinct from my own was just something I was going to have to accept. I couldn't think of a simple energy exchange between humans that would make one noticeably more powerful, but Az insisted that I would benefit from it too, and honestly, it was clear from the fact that I wasn't still completely unconscious that Az wasn't lying about that part. I was beyond exhausted, my body ached with it. I could feel my brain trying to shut things down, even now. One kiss had been enough to bring me back from unconsciousness, and I didn't feel like any part of me was missing. Az was talking about making me stronger… and they had made it perfectly clear that if they just wanted to take my soul they didn't need my permission. Az wanted to help me, and damn it all, I needed help.

"Does it hurt?" I asked, finally willing myself to admit that I might have to do this if I wanted to be a functional person anytime soon.

It was Azrael's turn to laugh then.

"Oh, Luv. Quite the opposite, I assure you. I am widely regarded as one of the best lovers in *any* realm, and I come by that reputation completely honestly. I guarantee you that not only will it not hurt, but it may well be the most pleasurable experience you've ever had."

The smile that accompanied that statement was enough to have me almost panting. I was seeing both Az's again, but I closed my eyes for a moment and decided to focus on the female Az. I opened my eyes and felt my pulse race and heat flood my body. There was no denying that the idea of getting *much* closer to Az was entirely appealing whenever I didn't think about the whole "taking part of my soul" piece.

"So, I get an energy boost and some healing out of it, and what do you get?" I asked, trying to shed the last of my hesitation. If I was going to do this, I wanted to enjoy it, and not be hung up on my random fears of the metaphysics behind it.

"Oh, Vic, Luv, you'll get quite a bit more than an energy boost, but I can't say what exactly, as we've never tangled before. Similarly, I can't tell you exactly what I'll get out of it either, outside of some fun with a person I respect and find very attractive. We will both take a piece of each other away with us. It doesn't bind us, if that's what you're worried about. We exchange energy, and a bit of… spirit, if you will? But nothing that marks either of us as a possession. It's important you understand that; this isn't like vampirism, or any of the more sordid demon exchanges. It's an even trade—the give and take must be equal. I know I'll give you enough energy and healing to make you fit for immediate action, but beyond that I can only guess based on our respective powers. Those will mix and come out magnified, possibly changed, on the other end, but it's anyone's guess as to how. I'm afraid there's really only one way to find out."

I took a deep breath. When it came down to it, I trusted Az. They'd had plenty of chances to do horrible things to me if they'd wanted to, and it sounded like they could have just forgone my consent if they wanted to be underhanded, and taken my energy without me ever knowing or caring until it was too late. I thought of the vampires that Az had dropped so easily when we'd rescued Siara, and a shiver went down my spine. If they were just here to hurt me, they'd be done by now. They weren't doing that, and ok, that alone did not make them a hero, but I trusted them. And I was willing to give up a little bit of spirit if it meant I could get back to making sure my friends didn't die while attempting to save the world.

"Alright," I said, trying to smile as I took in the glory that was Azrael in any form; ebon skin, silver wings, white hair, silver eyes, and in this case, their deliciously feminine form. "Come show me why they call you the best succubus in all the realms."

Az's smile sent heat spreading through my whole body, and their approach was enough like that of a stalking cat to make me giggle nervously. Their eyes were so alight with heat and attraction as they approached the bed that all self-consciousness fled me, scars, spirit, and exhaustion all forgotten.

"I promise you will never regret this choice, Victoria Marmot," they purred, as they spread their wings and bent down to envelope me in a kiss so electric I was fairly certain my hair was standing on end afterwards.

~~~

What felt like hours and a hundred climaxes later, when we came back to reality, we were both glowing. Literally. Silver light radiated from both Az's skin and my own, and I watched in fascination as the air around us trembled with unspent energy. I felt alive. I felt like I'd just climbed a 14er and
~~~

simultaneously gotten twelve hours of solid sleep. This was somehow more than that, though. I felt like I could almost see time. My senses were sharper than they'd ever been, as though I was part snow leopard, part dragon, and part myself all at once. So much had happened in the short time that Az and I had been intimate that it all sort of melted together, but there had been a few key moments when I'd felt like we had ceased being two separate entities. It was every trite romance novel description of a climax, except it was more than a metaphor, it had felt like our bodies, and our perceptions, had actually become a single unit for a series of heartbeats. At the time, it had seemed like the only logical outcome of the way we'd joined our bodies, but afterwards it was clearly more than that. Something in me felt altered. I was more than I had been at the start.

"Wow."

Az's voice caused my head to snap up from where I'd been staring at my own hands and contemplating the difference I felt.

"I thought you'd done this a hundred times," I said, watching them flex their wings and stare at their own hands on the bed next to me.

"This is…different than the last few exchanges I've done," Az admitted, still staring at their hands.

"Is the glowing not normal, then?" I asked, suddenly worried.

"Not exactly," said Az. "It's cool, though. I can't wait to see what new tricks we've picked up."

"New tricks?" I asked, now nervously watching Az's wide-eyed expression, as they inspected their own skin.

"Yeah. I did mention the part about growing stronger, didn't I?" Az finally met my eyes with an expression of genuine puzzlement.

"Yes, you said you'd get stronger, but—"

"Not just me, Luv. You too. This was an exchange—couldn't you feel it? We've both gained something. I just can't tell what yet. It will be truly delightful to find out."

I took a deep breath. Right. For Az this was a neat science experiment. For me, it was a healing I desperately needed and… well, boy howdy, had it ever worked. I not only felt like I had the energy to get up and walk, I almost felt like I had enough energy to fly without my dragon wings. It was… mildly disconcerting, but only because I felt like I needed to go run a few miles before I burst at the seams.

"Shall we go kick some MOME ass, then?" I asked, unable to contain myself any longer.

Az smiled widely and nodded.

"Oh yes. Let's."

THE LAST PERSON I had expected to find waiting outside the room in which I had just had very vigorous and probably quite vocal sex with a succubus was Albert, but if my life randomly started meeting my expectations now, I was going to get incredibly suspicious.

Az and I walked into Rhelia's living room to find the white-haired mage enjoying a cup of tea and a magazine on Rhelia's largest sofa.

"Everyone feeling better now?" he asked, without preamble.

I felt the blood run to my cheeks and ears, and tried to remember that what we'd just done had been the only way to get me back on my feet in time to be useful to our plans, though it was difficult to remember that now, after however much time we'd spent decidedly *not* hurrying the experience.

"Yes," I said, my voice clearer and stronger than I'd expected it to be. "I'm ready to get to work on stopping MOME and Dryer. Have the dragons already launched their attack?"

Albert shook his head.

"No, they agreed to wait the ten minutes I assured them it would take to have you in fighting shape."

"Ten minutes?" I asked, looking between Az and Albert with my eyebrows shooting up to high five in the middle of my forehead.

"Yes, I managed to put that room into a brief temporal distortion. Azrael assured me that three hours would be enough, and I managed to slip you out of time enough for that to take only a few minutes. We wouldn't have needed the full ten if we hadn't had to carry you over here. Still, we'd best get back to the field if we are going to launch our attack in time to catch Dryer unawares."

If I hadn't just spent Gwen-knew-how-many hours or days trapped in my own pocket di-mension, and then come back to the exact instant I left, I would have assumed that Albert was making a very bad joke, or had simply lost his mind. As it was, I understood exactly how he could have used his dark matter to keep us suspended in our own timeline outside of this one, and so I simply nodded and reached my hand out to take his proffered one. Az took my other hand, and then I blinked us into existence in front of General Aira.

~~~

I was almost giddy with how little energy it had taken for me to move the three of us from Rhelia's home to the middle of the dragon council's plateau. Granted, it was a tiny distance, relatively speaking, but still, yesterday it would have been a noticeable drain on my energy to carry the three of us that far, and now it felt like I'd barely blinked. I wanted to laugh at how little it had cost me. If this was what getting busy with Azrael did for me, I was going to have to seriously reconsider my 'no giving part of your soul to succubi' stance. I felt like I could move a mountain with nothing more than my big toe.

Instead I tried to arrange my face into something resembling a grave expression. General Aira was going over her attack plan with Albert, as he suggested how we might maneuver our strike team to take out Dryer.
~~~

"She'll be hiding, in all likelihood," Albert explained. "It's unlikely that she'll be among any of her people at MOME, least of all wherever she plans to set someone off using Technetium next. She won't want to be in the line of fire. Hers, or ours."

"So how do we find her?" Azrael asked.

I remained silent, but my brain started to throw together a number of puzzle pieces, even as Albert began to speak.

"We'll have to hope she's at one of her known hideouts and send multiple strike teams timed exactly with our other attacks."

General Aira was shaking her head.

"We don't have time for that. We can't assume that she won't hear about those strike teams before one of them actually reaches her, so we would risk putting her on high alert instead of taking her by surprise. We can't take the risk that she'll predict our movements and take out our best people after the first strike force is discovered."

"We can't just do nothing," Albert said, voice rising, as though this wasn't the first time General Aira had rebuffed him. "Dryer is the linchpin to this whole operation. If we don't remove her, none of this will ever stop. We've got to—"

"Albert," I interrupted, my brain taking over my mouth before any other part of me could think better of it. "Do you have any way to get some of Rebecca's blood?"

Albert and the general looked at me, their faces almost humorous mirrors of surprise, but Azrael smiled, as though they knew what I was thinking.

"I am not in the habit of keeping the blood of my enemies on my person," Albert replied, calmly.

"Well, do you know where we might find a relative of hers? One that's not under the same kind of security that she is?"

Albert thought for a moment.

"I might be able to find a cousin of hers. We were friends in school, and we've kept in touch over the years."

"Excellent," I replied, unable to keep the smile off my face. "Then if you'll just give me a few minutes, I believe I have a plan."

STANDING ON A very narrow ledge with a three thousand foot drop behind me should have been terrifying. Even years of rock climbing, and my latest forays into free-climbing, hadn't changed that. What *had* changed was that I now felt exhilarated by the height, the danger, and the energy pulsing through me that was practically urging me to jump and see if I could really fly without wings right now. That little voice was terrifying, so I closed my eyes against the view of distant green meadows dotted with needle towers and embraced by a hazy mountain range, took a deep breath filled with clean late summer air, and then turned towards the whole reason I'd come here.

The cell in front of me was bare stone, fronted by iron bars as thick as my arm, and sparsely furnished. It contained what looked like a recently cleaned latrine in one corner, a small bookshelf covered in withered paperbacks, and a low, but clean and comfortable looking, pallet. Atop the pallet was what looked like an enormous pile of stacked cowhides.

"To what do I owe the pleasure, Ms. Marmot?" asked a baritone voice originating from the center of the pile.

"I've come to ask a favor," I replied.

The pile of cowhides sat up, revealing itself to be a single cowhide draped across a large, muscular man covered in short brown fur and topped with a bull's head.

"I am listening," Torrence replied.

"Is Nethia…" my voice trailed off, unsure of how to word the rest of my question.

"She has not woken since you last saw her. I have been informed that she is being kept somewhere comfortable yet secure, and if she ever wakes, she will stand trial for her crimes."

I swallowed. I wasn't sure which was worse, honestly, an unending magical coma brought on by a broken blood oath, or whatever the dragons were likely to do to her when she was finally put on trial.

"I'm sorry," I managed to say after a moment. "I know you were…friends."

Torrence sighed and stood up from the pallet, walking over to the bars beside me and leaning against them.

"Once, perhaps. I am afraid Nethia and I haven't been friends for a long time now. The bond of the Dragon Hunters was all that held us anymore, and she made it clear that even that meant little to her in the end. I thought, hoped is perhaps more accurate, that she had seen the wrong in all that we had done, as I had."

Torrence stared into the distance. The view through the bars was unencumbered, and certainly good for contemplation. Leave it to the dragons to put their prison inside the tallest cliff in the realm. Maybe they were hoping the view would inspire their prisoners to lead better lives. Or maybe they just wanted to terrify people. With dragons it was hard to know. Maybe I just needed to spend more time as a dragon to figure it out.

"I was wrong, regardless. She was very good at convincing the world, or at least the Unterberg council, that she believed in the values that Unterberg strives for and—"

"Look, Torrence, I don't want to keep you from mourning Nethia in your own way, but my favor is kind of…time sensitive."

I grimaced. I really hated to interrupt the dude while he was processing this, but I'd barely managed to convince General Aira to hold off her attack while I enacted my "plan," and I'd never told her what I was planning to do, just that I had a way to get to Dryer that would let us keep the element of surprise. She'd reluctantly agreed, with Albert's added prodding. I'd only gotten away with not telling her the details because she wanted it done fast, and didn't want to waste time on planning sessions. Luckily, with my particular skill set, I didn't really need her to know what I was up to.

"If I could get the dragons to reduce your sentence, would you be willing to help me track someone again?"

"Is it to aid in stopping MOME?" Torrence asked, his large brown eyes on me now, instead of staring into the distance.

"Yes," I replied.

"Then there is no need to ask the dragons to reduce my sentence. I will gladly help."

My mouth snapped shut in surprise. I'd been about to admit I wasn't sure how much I could do.

I didn't really have the authority to do anything for Torrence's sentence, I was just banking on the hope that speaking for him when his trial came would help reduce his sentence.

The more I got to know Torrence, the more I realized that I didn't understand him at all. Who the fuck just volunteers to help the folks who have them imprisoned and refuses to get their punishment reduced? He'd said before that he regretted his past, but hell, lots of people said that, and some of them meant it, too. Meaning it and embracing retribution seemed like two vastly different things to me, though. Still, whether or not I understood Torrence, I was starting to like him. He seemed…honorable. Plus, how could you dislike someone who frolicked in wildflowers at the drop of a hat?

So I smiled when I reached out a hand towards his.

"Shake on it?" I asked.

He tilted his large, horned head to one side and eyed my hand suspiciously before reaching out his own deep brown, furred one.

As soon as his skin hit mine, I pulled us both through time and space.

W E BLINKED INTO existence at the bottom of the valley, not far from where I'd left Albert and General Aira only minutes before. Indeed, General Aira was seated a few meters away, in her human form, her legs folded beneath her and a rather elaborate tea set spread out before her. She was alone, which I supposed I should have expected. After all, I knew that Albert needed to track down the blood we'd talked about. But it was probably the first time I hadn't seen General Aira swamped by dragons in all forms, asking her questions and giving reports, as she orchestrated what she had informed me was the largest fighting force of dragons assembled in over a century. I hesitated before approaching her, since she seemed to be enjoying the uncommon moment of calm.

Then I noticed Trev, Rhelia, Sol, and Seamus all huddled up a few meters away from Aira's tea ceremony. The group turned as one when we moved towards them, and Seamus and Trev immediately came over to us to give Torrence a quick fist bump and say hello.

My eyebrows must have arched in curiosity, because Trev communicated silently, *We all wound up fighting together once you and Sol made it into the dungeons. Torrence fought like a master. He's kind of a badass.*

Oh. Right.

Of course there had been a whole battle after we'd managed to rescue Siara. It only made sense that they'd have to fight their way out after I had whisked Siara to the only place I could think of where she wouldn't blow up the entire universe. So much had happened to me since then, I almost forgot that everyone else had been rescuing Siara just yesterday. For me, it had been a week, several worlds, and a dimensional pocket ago. For everyone standing around me, it had been last night.

I restrained a sigh, and longed for, of all people, Az. They, at least, had been with me for the bulk of what happened after Siara's rescue. Meanwhile, I hadn't even had a chance to tell everyone else what had happened, except in the broadest terms.

While I stood there feeling strangely isolated, even while surrounded by my friends, Torrence seemed genuinely concerned about everyone's health and well-being. He was even asking Seamus about how his Moms were settling into life in Unterberg.

Which is probably why none of us noticed the sound of steel being drawn. Or the sound of a blade cutting through air. Until the blade was buried in Torrence's chest, and his legs collapsed beneath him.

Trev and I were instantly at Torrence's side, while Rhelia turned, yellow eyes flashing as she sought out the enemy.

Which turned out to be the petite dragon General a few meters away, glaring at our group as though we were all demons of the worst kind.

"How dare you remove a prisoner from their cell?!" she shrieked. It was a sharp contrast to the calm tones she'd maintained through every conversation I'd heard with her yet. Even when she completely disagreed with people, her tone was, at worst, calmly dismissive. Now she was shouting at full volume, and when I took a brief moment to glance her way, I saw her eyes wide, whites showing prominently, and spittle flying from the corners of her mouth. "What would possess you to release that kind of menace on my realm? Have you lost your minds? Do you know what he could have done to us? Do you have any idea what his kind are capable of?"

I barely registered the words, because I was too busy fighting to keep Torrence's blood in his body. It was a battle I was losing rapidly. The wakizashi that had been launched though his chest had been aimed with uncanny precision. His heart had been skewered. His eyes were already closed, and I could feel no pulse.

Trev, I sent silently, because if what I was about to do didn't work, he was my best chance at plan B. *Grab on.*

I was already holding Torrence, and as soon as I felt Trev's hand hit my shoulder, I reached to the one place that had always been there to save my ass in the past.

IN AN INSTANT, we were both blinking in the dappled light of a small clearing in the Northern Arizona woods.

"WHY ARE YOU BACK SO SOON, VICTORIA?"

"Life, can you save him?" I asked, skipping past all preamble, ignoring the fact that Life's definition of "so soon" and mine were probably vastly different, and hoping against hope that Torrence wasn't already dead, at least not the level of dead that Life couldn't fix. I didn't know if Trev's phoenix fire would be enough to work on someone I barely knew. I had a feeling it had only worked on Sol because we'd already gotten close enough for me to use our mating bond to help call her spirit back, but I'd be damned if I wouldn't try it anyway, if it came to that.

"THE BOVINE IS ALREADY HEALING," Life replied, tilting his hooded head to one side. "HE WAS BARELY ATTACHED TO HIS LIFE FORCE, HOWEVER. A FEW MORE SECONDS AND HE WOULD HAVE BEEN BEYOND MY HELP. WHAT DID YOU DO TO HIM?"

I looked down at Torrence and saw that, indeed, the wakizashi had been ejected from his flesh and the wound was already knitting closed in its wake.

I sighed, collapsing to the ground. The shift from the dragon realm to here hadn't taken anything out of me, really, even with Trev and Torrence in tow—thank you, Azrael—but the adrenaline leaving my system left my legs shaky, even without the drain on my power.

"I didn't do anything to him except bring him here," I said, as I caught my breath. "A pissed-off dragon threw a sword at him."

Life didn't have a face that I could see, beyond the two glowing orbs that marked his eyes within the wooden hood of his cloak, but I could have sworn he was frowning anyway.

"FRIENDSHIP WITH YOU APPEARS TO BE A VERY HIGH RISK FACTOR FOR THE HEALTH OF OTHERS."

I laughed, though a part of me wanted to cry.

"I can't argue with that," I muttered, leaning back against one of the nearby trees.

After a few deep breaths of fresh mountain air tinged with the sweet scent of butterscotch pines, and a moment of staring in silence at the woods that surrounded the small open clearing of the Tree of Life, I looked at Trev. As soon as our eyes met, I felt a pang of guilt; it was probably the first time I'd *really* looked at him since I'd come back from my own dimensional pocket.

"Hey," he said, sitting down against the tree beside me.

"Hey," I replied, eloquence escaping me entirely.

He reached his hand out towards mine, but hesitated before our fingers met. I looked at him, frowned, and grabbed his hand from where it hovered a few inches from mine.

"I'm sorry," we said in unison. Then we both laughed.

"Yeah," I said, giving his hand a squeeze. "I don't know why you kept Mom and Dad a secret, but I'm going to go out on a limb and guess that it was for some noble reason."

"I didn't want them kicked out of the Realm of the Dead," he said quietly.

"You think Hel would boot them, just because I knew they were alive?" I asked, one eyebrow arching incredulously.

He shrugged.

"They said the only reason it was safe to tell *me* where they were was that I was dead to the people who had known me."

I stared at him.

"They sent me an e-mail, Vic. I don't even know how they sent an e-mail from a different realm, but they did, and that was the only communication I had from them for ages and then…. Well, after everyone thought Rhelia was dead, she was able to go visit them, so…I found out a bit more then."

"You couldn't go visit them?" I asked.

"I probably could have if I'd gone back before I found you, but… after that I was alive again, at least to the people who loved me, and maybe even as soon as I replied to Mom and Dad. I don't know exactly how it works. But no, I couldn't go see them. But Rhelia *could*, even though you and I technically knew she was still alive… it seems like a weird set of rules, if you ask me."

I shrugged. "We might have known she was alive, but we'd doubted it for a bit, and EVERY-ONE else thought she was dead. I mean, a large number of people believed that very firmly, and still do. Maybe that's all it takes."

"Did Mom and Dad tell you why they left?" Trev asked, his voice quiet.

"Not really," I said, leaning my head back farther against the tree. I was too embarrassed to explain that I hadn't given them a chance to explain anything. Although I wasn't sure Hel would have let them talk to me, even if I'd been more cooperative.

"Well, we should—"

"We should be getting back to Albert's office," rumbled a deep, now-becoming-familiar voice.

"Torrence!" I said, launching to my feet.

The large tauren was standing up, looking decidedly healthy for someone who had basically died a few minutes ago.

"Vic, Trevor, I am deeply indebted to you both. I would not have survived that attack were it not for your quick thinking and incredible facility with teleporting."

Trev waved his hands up as though fending off the praise.

"I didn't do anything," he said. "I was just here as plan B."

Torrence looked slightly puzzled, but nodded.

"And you don't owe me shit," I said, smiling and giving him a hug. He stood awkwardly still for a moment, then wrapped his large furry arms around me in return. "I'm just happy you're alive."

"Regardless, I owe you my life."

"Ugh, fine. You owe me your life. I'll try to figure out a way for you to pay me back without dying, 'kay?"

Torrence simply stared at me.

"You need to lighten up, Torrence."

Torrence frowned.

"YOU ARE DISTURBING MY PEACEFUL GLEN, VICTORIA AND FRIENDS."

Honestly, that whole day was almost made worthwhile by the sight of Torrence nearly jumping out of his skin at the sound of Life's voice.

"Sorry, Life. We'll get out of your hair. Life, this is Torrence. Torrence, Life. Life is really the one you ought to be thanking, Torrence. I just brought you here. Life did the hard part."

"DO NOT LISTEN TO THE HUMAN. I CANNOT HELP BUT MEND THAT WHICH STILL HAS LIFE TO LEND IT. I WOULD LITERALLY HAVE DONE THE SAME FOR ANYONE. I EVEN HEALED THAT OB-NOXIOUS VAMPIRE THAT KEPT COM-

ING BACK HERE UNTIL VIC IMMOLATED HIS HEAD. THEN I COULD NO LONGER MEND HIM. THAT WAS SATISFACTORY."

Torrence, not seeming nearly as composed as he'd been a moment earlier, sketched a formal bow towards the large talking tree, and then quickly turned back to us.

"May we go now?" he asked quietly.

I decided to take pity on him, since Life can be a bit much when you're not expecting him, and I grabbed Torrence and Trevor by the wrists and blinked us to where I hoped we would find Albert and a vial of blood.

LBERT'S OFFICE WAS empty when we reached it, save for two disgruntled-looking iguanas who hissed angrily at us when we popped into existence in the middle of their lair. The place looked pretty much exactly as it had the last time I'd been there, including the faint smell of weed permeating the elaborate throw rugs that sat beneath Albert's desk, and the two wingback chairs.

"Where are we?" Torrence asked, after a moment.

"Albert's office," I replied. "He said he'd meet me here after he got ahold of what he needed, so——"

"Ah. Vic, Trevor, lovely to see you. Torrence, it has been…some time."

We all turned to see Albert standing just in front of the door that led into the Flagstaff High School main corridor, though I was fairly certain Albert hadn't used the door.

"Indeed it has," Torrence replied. There was something oddly delicate about the way that they were addressing each other, which made me curious about how they knew each other, but there was no time for that now.

"Did you get it?" I asked

In response, Albert pulled a small vial of red liquid from a pocket tucked away in the thick, robe-like overcoat he always wore.

"Rebecca's cousin seemed all too happy to help, when I asked. Seems they aren't on the best of terms these days."

Yet another topic I would love to ask more about, but we really didn't have the time.

"Can you two complete the ritual without us?" I asked, gesturing between me and Trev, who hadn't said a word since we'd arrived here. Albert and Torrence both nodded. "Albert, Torrence will have to stay with you. Nethia could have cast this spell on an object, but Torrence can only make himself a compass. Is that ok?"

Albert shrugged, as if he would make do with what he got.

"We should probably be getting back to see what the hell is wrong with General Aira," I added.

"Why should anything be wrong with General Aira?" Albert asked.

I sighed.

"Because she threw a wakizashi through Torrence's heart without so much as saying hello first. Still not clear on why, since we were too busy taking Torrence to Life to make sure he didn't die. Maybe… consider not returning him to the dragon realm when you two are done."

"I will return to the dragon realm to face my crimes and receive justice," Torrence declared.

"Ok…your call. We have to go. Good luck finding Dryer. I'll tell General Aira that you two are on the mission we'd planned, and she can yell at me all she wants. Hopefully without any swords, though."

Then, before Albert or Torrence could object, I grabbed Trev's hand in mine, felt a rush of warmth from the thought that things were mending between us, then closed my eyes and reached for a sunny valley filled with dragons and wildflowers.

UT THE SUNNY valley filled with dragons and wildflowers appeared to be in absolute chaos.

I had taken us back to the spot where I'd last seen General Aira, hoping to find her in a calmer mood. General Aira was there, but so was everyone else, apparently. Twenty people or more surrounded the dragon general, all trying to speak at once, while the troops still massed on the field around us shifted anxiously, as though awaiting the final order to attack. I was honestly surprised that General Aira, currently in her dragon form, hadn't started biting people's heads off, just so she could actually hear people over the din.

I won't lie, after what had happened with Torrence, I hesitated to approach the General in her dragon form, even though all the evidence suggested she was just as deadly in her human one. I scanned the crowd around Aira, hoping to find backup in the form of Rhelia. I didn't see her.

Trev and I were still holding hands when I picked two other familiar figures out of the crowd, though, and that may have been the only thing that kept me upright.

"Is that…?" Trev asked, squeezing my fingers in his.

"Yes," I replied, my voice cracking slightly.

And then we were both running for our Mom and Dad.

In that moment, I forgot about the lies, forgot about the abandonment, pushed aside every negative thought I'd had about my parents in the past year. They were here. They were alive, and in front of me, and not trapped in some strange dimension that I could only visit if everyone thought I was dead.

Trev and I ran, and for a moment, in the middle of a crowd of people trying to organize a war, our world narrowed to a tangle of arms and chests as we somehow managed to all hug each other at once.

"How are you here?" I asked, between hugs, trying to look at both my Mom's and Dad's faces at the same time. "How did you get away from

Hel? I thought she was planning to keep you as collateral until I got back?"

"You managed to convince her that the fight against MOME was more important than whatever petty plans she had for a power grab," my Mom replied, hugging me again, crushing my face to her shoulder and then holding me out at arm's length. "After you left, we told her that we had to get to you as soon as possible, that if you were going to succeed in stopping MOME you had to know what we knew."

Dad finally let go of Trev long enough to talk, even as he wiped away the tears from his eyes and cheeks.

"We have to get Albert and General Aira to listen. You can't go after Dryer."

"Dad, we have to go after her. If we don't stop her, we don't stop any of this. MOME will just keep coming after us," I said, exasperated. "Besides, Albert is already gone."

"True, but I don't mean that no one should go after Dryer, only that *you* shouldn't. Let Albert handle Dryer, he can handle her alone. *You* need to go after the Technetium itself."

"Why issss that?" asked a sibilant voice from behind us.

We turned to see that General Aira, and all of the various commanders who had shown up to complain, demand, and wait, had gone silent and turned to look at us.

"Respectfully, General Aira, if we don't remove the Technetium before Dryer knows she's under attack, she'll just make sure we never find it. If she does that, we'll never be able to neutralize it, and this fight will go on forever."

"Are you saying you can neutralize the Technetium?" I asked, my voice flat with the shock of it.

Mom and Dad both nodded, looking around at the assembled group.

"It's why we disappeared, the whole reason we faked our own deaths. We've been looking for a way to neutralize Technetium for decades, but we finally realized that the answer didn't exist in this realm. Once we realized that we needed to go to the Realm of the Dead to finish our research, we knew we would have to fake our deaths and have *everyone* believe it."

Mom and Dad both turned to look regretfully at me, and I stamped down hard on the anger that started to surge up inside me. I could be angry with them later—right now I was going to have to listen to what they had to say, so that we could all live long enough to be moody with each other tomorrow.

"We do not have time for thissss," said General Aira. "We musssst ready our attack before word of our preparationssss reachessss the Minisssstry of Magical Entitiessss."

Mom nodded, but kept talking, "Right. So we won't go into how we figured out how to neutralize Technetium, we'll just tell you that we did, and that we've brought enough serum to neutralize what we hope is the entirety of MOME's stock."

"Even if we neutralize all the Technetium they have, what's to stop them from just making more?" asked Trev, looking skeptical.

It was Dad who answered.

"How about a bunch of dragons completely destroying their labs and all of their research?"

A gleam appeared in General Aira's enormous eyes as she said, "Indeed, that may jussst do the trick."

"As long as we can find all of their research and storage facilities," I said, trying to rein in the hope that was starting to surge through me. Could we really do this? Could it be this easy?

"We already know where they are," said Mom.

O F COURSE, WHEN Mom said they knew where the Technetium stores were, what she really meant was that she had a highly educated guess as to where they were, because, of course, she had been trapped in the Realm of the Dead for the last year (at least according to our timeline—according to their timeline, Mom and Dad had been in the Realm of the dead for more like five years, a number that didn't match up exactly with my own experience of time there, but at least was similarly distorted) and thus they hadn't been able to confirm their hypothesis.

Still, as I stood in the dank tunnel leading down to my "favorite" dungeon, breathing in the unfortunately familiar scent of stale water, moss, and burning torches, I couldn't fault their reasoning.

Technetium was deadly, if given half a chance to mix with dark matter, and dark matter was damned near everywhere, so the only safe place to store it was in a place that suppressed dark matter. And MOME had access to a handful of such places, namely the dungeons beneath all of their major headquarters. (I guess it shouldn't be surprising that an organization that claimed responsibility for policing all magical entities would have a bunch of dark matter suppressing dungeons, but it still seemed like a weird architectural quirk to me.)

The trick, of course, was getting to all of those places, as well as the research facilities, and Dryer, all at the same time. It didn't have to be down to the second, since we figured it was unlikely that Dryer was so well prepared that a single second of notice would ruin our attempts, but by our best calculations we couldn't allow for more than a minute of lag between all of the attacks, or else we ran the risk of one location warning all the others and giving them time to clear out before we could do what we came to do. Which was why I had zipped back to Flagstaff as soon as General Aira had agreed to the wait, and thankfully caught Albert and Torrence right after they'd finished the blood magic ceremony that would allow them to track Dryer. I'd told them just enough to make sure our timing would work out, and then I'd gone straight to MOME's Phoenix HQ dungeons. Trev and Rhelia insisted that now that they had a device inside of the security system (they'd confirmed it was still there after our adventure rescuing Siara), they could make the system ignore the breach my shifting in would cause. They could turn the alarm trigger into an error message, buying me enough time to get past the security feeds before we started blowing shit up.

It was an intense plan, and I hated the fact that it required all of us splitting up. I'd been tempted to transport everyone into position by using my newly supercharged powers. I still wasn't feeling any noticeable drain, despite all the shifting I'd done today already, but my parents had, rather sensibly, insisted that I should save whatever stores I had for the mission, rather than wasting it all on setup. After all, we were lining up attacks in seven major cities around the world, all of which we suspected held sufficient stores of Technetium to blow up the world several times over, and I was probably going to need my A-game just to get through this. We had other mages that could shift people, and dragons that could fly, and one or two magical objects that rendered folks invisible. It would be unnecessary for me to take all of my friends to the places they were needed.

Fair enough.

I was in position, keeping an eye on my phone for timing while simultaneously working on calming the panic that threatened to well up inside me as I contemplated the last time that I'd been here.

A few deep breaths helped, as did imagining what Sol, Seamus, Trev, and Rhelia would be doing. They should each be reaching their targets about now. Seamus had been given the task of tackling the now "abandoned" Bolivian HQ, on the assumption that it would be the least heavily guarded. Even still, he'd been given a few were-dragons for backup. Sol, meanwhile, had been placed at the European HQ, in the hope that her intricate knowledge of MOME's workings might get her well into the facility without attracting notice before she drew attention by wrecking the place. Trev and Rhelia had been sent together to take on the MOME HQ in Shanghai, because Rhelia thought she had a contact there, but none of us were sure enough about that to risk her going without backup. Albert had been sent with Torrence (who we were referring to as "the compass" in front of General Aira, until further notice) to go after Rebecca Dryer, wherever she wound up being, and Azrael and General Aira were both coordinating troops to attack the research facilities as soon as we cleared the Technetium stores. Because, of course, most of the research facilities were in the same compounds as the storage facilities for Technetium, since they all required dark matter suppression to function without blowing everyone up. 'Cause my life has never been easy enough that we wouldn't have to worry about roasting me and all of my friends alive, after we neutralized the Technetium, if we didn't get things exactly right.

The timing was going to be delicate, to say the least.

I, for one, had been all in favor of just blowing up the Technetium stores, along with everything else, but it had quickly been pointed out to me that doing so risked exposing the Technetium stores to dark matter, thus *causing* the very giant, world-ending explosions that we'd been worried about to begin with.

Nothing's ever easy, is it?

So, now, after checking my watch and seeing my start time tick by with my heart in my damned mouth, I was sneaking my way down into the dungeons on foot, hoping that I didn't run into enough guards to set off the alarms before I got to wherever the Technetium was hidden. I couldn't rely on Trev and Rhelia to help, now that the start time had passed. They had remote access on their phones, but there was no guarantee that they wouldn't be busy with their own problems, or lose signal.

The first guard was pretty easy.

She didn't see me coming. She was busy wrestling with her keys, and didn't even have her footing properly when I hit her in the back of the head. I managed to catch her before she collapsed, and then I very carefully and respectfully took her out of her uniform (thankfully she was wearing shorts and a T-shirt underneath, so I didn't feel like too much of a creeper—even still, I laid my clothes on top of her out of a weird sense of "fairness"), and then I donned the stolen jumpsuit, complete with belt, keys, and baton, before tucking her into the first empty cell I could find. And ok, just because I did it respectfully doesn't mean it was cool, because obviously I didn't have her consent, but I was trying to save the world, and we were both going to have to just live with it. I hadn't had her consent for knocking her out either, but I didn't have time to convince everyone at MOME to join the side of reason before they blew up the world. It was going to have be enough for now.

Even wearing a MOME uniform, I had to hope that I wouldn't run into many other guards. I didn't think my disguise would get me very far if I ran into anyone who worked with her.

I'd made it to the third cell down the ramp when I saw two faces I'd never really expected to see again.

"Sylvestra?" I thought hard, but couldn't come up with the Troll's name, and wasn't sure I'd ever heard it before. I decided it was safest to just skip ahead. "What are you two doing here? I thought you were free of MOME after La Paz."

Sylvestra flew up to the bars that enclosed the cell, and I noticed that the whole cell front had been lined with some sort of mesh, probably meant to keep the pixie contained, since she was more than small enough to fit between the bars.

"You're Rhelia's friend, yes?" said the large troll who leaned against the back wall of the cell.

"Yeah. What happened to you two?" I asked again, completely baffled as to how they'd wound up here, of all places. The last time I'd seen them they'd kindly ignored us (after a brief misunderstanding) as we rescued Rhelia from the MOME dungeons in the Andean HQ. Unless they'd stuck around for some reason, they should have been free and clear of MOME and their shenanigans. We'd certainly left the place in enough turmoil for everyone who'd been looking for an excuse to slip away.

The troll shrugged.

"MOME tracked us down for guard duty again. We thought maybe they didn't know how the last one ended, so we said yes. Turns out it was just a trap."

He said it with the kind of tone that suggested this was just the sort of thing that happened in his life. Nothing to be worried about. Sylvestra, meanwhile, just buzzed angrily in the air in front of me. I shook my head, reminding myself that I was on a seriously tight schedule. Before I even started speaking, I began sorting through the keys on my belt.

"Well, my friends, today is your lucky day, as long as you can restrain yourselves from wreaking havoc until you get clear of this place entirely. I'm afraid that this time through we're shooting for stealth, and we're on a tight schedule."

"Do you spend all of your time breaking in and out of MOME headquarters, then?" asked the troll.

I couldn't help but chuckle.

"It kinda feels like it, to be honest. Some days, it really does."

It didn't take too long for me to find the key that worked on their lock. As soon as the door popped open and I shifted it on its enormous hinges, Sylvestra drew her sword and charged me.

"Hey, what the fuck!? I just let you go, what's your problem?"

She sheathed her sword, but glared at me.

"You are my problem, human."

I blinked and looked between Sylvestra and the troll.

"Don't mind her, she's just cranky," he said. "She hates getting captured."

The troll held out a hand to me.

"Name's Cronk, by the way."

"Nice to meet you, Cronk. Call me Vic."

His handshake was firm, but for someone whose hand covered my entire arm, it was impressive that he managed to be so gentle. Then he turned away with a nod, beckoning to his miniature friend.

"Did they really just set you up to capture you?" I asked, somewhat befuddled as to why MOME would bother.

"Seems that way," Cronk said, still waiting for the pixie to fly away from me and towards the tunnel that would lead them out of here. "Guess we must have gone up the charts of 'most wanted' after we helped you lot escape the first time. The arse who locked us up kept muttering about us joining the right side, whether we wanted to or not."

He shrugged, then dropped his hand and glared at the pixie.

"Come on, Sylvestra. Let's get out of here before our new friend blows the whole place up."

Sylvestra shot me another haughty look, then turned to fly after the already departing troll.

"That reminds me," I called, as they hurried up the slope. "We really are blowing the place up this time. On purpose, I mean. I recommend hustling out of here and not making a fuss, if you can help it. We've got a lot riding on this one. Fate of the world, yada yada."

Cronk waved a giant hand to show that he'd heard and continued up the stone steps back towards the tunnel entrance I'd just come down. I turned and headed farther into the depths, hoping that I hadn't just ruined our entire plan by releasing a cranky pixie and a thoughtful troll.

IT WASN'T UNTIL I got past the tenth dungeon cell—all of which were now empty, even though three of them had been occupied before I came clanking down the tunnels with my stolen keyring of potential freedom—that I began to worry that there was never any Technetium stored in this particular dungeon after all.

The dripping stone walls of the steeply descending hall seemed to only be getting narrower and darker, and the smell of moss and wet stone was getting more and more overwhelming. I was officially farther into the dungeons than I'd ever been, and I had a hard time imagining that there was some kind of recently used storage facility below me. If anything, it seemed more likely that any door I might find would hide a centuries old cellar filled with gunpowder and wine casks, but none of the doors I'd opened on the way down here had contained stores of anything other than people that MOME considered criminals, so I'd continued to play Robin Hood and plough onwards.

Finally, I came across a low iron door that only came up to my chest, tucked awkwardly under what looked to be a natural arch in the rock. The hall continued on, but I could no longer see any torchlight flickering in its depths, and I wondered if anything lay in that direction. I kind of hoped not, although it would be strange for the hall to continue to nothing. Maybe it was just an emergency exit? Regardless, I really wanted this door to be the door I was looking for. I didn't want to have to keep going, or risk getting blown up when the dragons took out the research facilities above me, because I'd taken too long freeing captives along the way or…

I took a deep breath and decided to stop thinking about all the things I didn't want to have happen.

Instead, I set about finding the key that would fit the lock in front of me.

I was still on my knees, struggling to fit various oddly shaped pieces of metal into the dangling padlock that looked at least a hundred years old, when I heard a shoe scrape the stone behind me.

"Oh good, you're already on your knees. That should save us some time."

The voice sounded vaguely familiar, and the southern accent set my teeth on edge, so I wasn't entirely surprised by the view when I turned around and found Rebecca Dryer standing in the middle of the tunnel directly behind me.

I was, however, a bit taken aback to find that she had a gun pointed at Albert's head.

HIT, SHIT, SHIT, shit, shit.

This was not good. This was very bad. This was on the list of worst things that could go wrong at this point in the plan. It might have even been at the top of that list.

Because standing before me was evidence that we were completely screwed. Not only had Albert *not* taken out Rebecca Dryer, indeed, Albert seemed to have had his ass handed to him by Rebecca Dryer, Torrence was nowhere in sight, Dryer clearly knew what we were up to, and she seemed all too willing to stop it. And even if all she did was slow us down too much, we were all going to get blown up if we didn't get out of here in about seven minutes.

And just to top everything off, she had a gun. And I did not.

"Well, fuck," I said aloud, raising my hands above my head and turning my whole body to face her, while standing up slowly.

"Indeed," Rebecca replied. "This doesn't seem to be going well for you. Though I must say, I'm impressed with how far you've come. I didn't think our security would be that easy to bypass. I'm really going to have to have a "talk" with my people after this."

She was smiling as she spoke, as if we were just catching up over a cup of coffee instead of having a showdown in the middle of a centuries-old dungeon. I wasn't sure if that was a southern thing, or a lawyer thing, but I wasn't a fan either way. Still, it could be used to my advantage.

"How did you find me?" I asked, hoping she came from the James Bond school of villainy. Honestly, it seemed like decent odds she would want to talk. After all, a truly efficient villain would have simply shot me in the back of the head and capped Albert the minute she'd gotten the upper hand on him, so clearly she needed one, or both, of us for something.

"Oh, I didn't, sweetheart. I mean, I just stumbled upon you, really. Once I caught this bitch snooping around my office, I knew something was wrong, but I really only came down here because I needed a dose of Technetium for our mutual friend here."

She gestured towards Albert with the gun and I winced, watching the barrel dig into the skin above his ear.

"Gwendamnit, I hate guns," I whispered.

"What's that, dear?" Dryer asked.

"I said, I hate guns."

Dryer laughed, still keeping the tip of her Glock pointed at Albert's temple.

"That's rich, coming from someone who shot and almost killed one of our best agents."

"Hating them and knowing how to use them are two different things, Rebecca," I gritted.

"Tsk, tsk, so angry. Guns have their uses. Too many of our kind get caught up in *only* using magic. They are unable to see the bigger picture. After all, think of the long-term benefits. Why, if we adopted non-magical weaponry *as well* as magic, we could easily be the dominant force in our realm. Think of how many people could be spared, if we didn't have to prove our might without modern weapons. A single nuclear warhead, and we would never have to waste another dragon on something as banal as bringing the non-magical humans in line. Can you imagine? But it was all I could do to convince the damned council that it was time we asserted our dominance over the humans *at all*. They'd never have given the idea a second thought if I had tried to force them to accept human weapons on top of everything else. Luckily, I was able to find a purely magical solution to the problem, and now everyone is on board. That said, I'm going to need you to move, Deary. I need to get into that storage unit. This one has a date with some Technetium."

Before I could even react to her strange monologue, she was marching Albert forward, and then, in a move that would make any Bond villain proud, she took a moment to point the gun at me while insisting that I step aside. I was so horrified to have the barrel pointed my way that I didn't react to the fact that she'd pulled it away from Albert's temple for a heartbeat. If I'd had a gun myself, that would have been the window I'd have used to shoot her, but as it was I could only watch in awful fascination as Albert raised his right elbow and sent it shooting hard and fast into Rebecca's nose. As soon as I'd seen Albert's momentum shift, I'd started to dive out of the line of fire, which probably saved my life, but it did not prevent the hot, awful pain of having a bullet drive its way into the flesh of my left shoulder.

"FUCK!" I exclaimed, with no small amount of feeling. "Does *anyone* at MOME ever learn proper gun safety?"

I was mostly shouting to distract myself from the pain, and to keep myself from passing out.

Deciding I really didn't want to get shot again, I launched myself at Dryer's knees, hoping to tackle her to the ground before she could get around to pulling the trigger again. I connected and she collapsed, something she had been half on her way to doing anyway, thanks to Albert breaking her nose with his elbow.

Albert snatched the gun from the floor and pointed it at Rebecca, whose arms I was working quickly to pin behind her back. Unfortunately, she seemed to have no interest in going down easy, broken nose or no. She bucked and kicked beneath me, and I was struggling to keep both of her arms pinned. The pain in my shoulder was spiking every time she moved. I was honestly amazed I could pin her at all, and had to assume my ability to grit through this was entirely thanks to the boost from Azrael.

Boost or not, though, it wasn't enough to keep me from screaming when Dryer somehow managed to buck her head up into my left shoulder, directly against the bullet wound. I managed to keep hold of her with my right arm, but my left arm went numb when she hit the wound, and I dropped her left arm as a result.

Before I could recover from the pain, she turned and jammed her thumb into the hole in my shoulder, causing me to scream once more. I didn't drop her right arm, though, and managed to use it to drag her off-balance and head butt her in her already-broken nose.

Dryer let out a scream of her own, then, but I had to give her points for tenacity when she just dug her thumb even farther into my shoulder wound and screamed in my face. I went down, and she took no time in launching herself at Albert.

Which was probably her biggest mistake.

Because Albert had apparently just been waiting for an opening in which he was unlikely to shoot me. And I was now a heap of pain on the floor.

The shot was deafening, somehow louder than the one that had hit me in the shoulder, or maybe it was just the stillness that followed that made it seem so loud. I tried not to let my stomach heave as the copper tang of blood mixed with the overwhelming stench of gunpowder in the tunnel around me.

"I d-didn't mean…" Albert stuttered, from where he stood. "I d-don't have much experience with guns."

"It's her fault for leaving the safety off," I said, trying to get my legs to respond to my brain. Which was kinda true, because honestly, what else did she expect was going to happen?

I didn't want to look at Dryer to see where she'd been shot, but I needed to walk past her to get to the storage unit, because we were even closer to getting immolated by dragon fire whether Dryer was dead or not. We were surrounded by dark matter suppressing stone, which, not surprisingly, also suppressed cell signal, and we had no way of letting General Aira know that she shouldn't light us up when the time came.

So, I shuffled past, and tried not to notice how still she was lying, or the pool of blood beneath her. I had to assume it was a head shot, since she'd stopped moving so quickly, but I really didn't want to find out. I kept my eyes on the old oak and iron gate, and the padlock that held it closed.

It didn't take long to fumble the lock open, but it felt like ages all the same.

The crate that sat in the middle of the long, arched storage room looked incongruously small, considering how much potential disaster it held within it.

"Is that it?" I asked, almost deflated. I don't know why I'd expected there to be more, but some part of me had thought the room would be packed wall-to-wall with the stuff.

"That's more than enough to take out Earth several times over, if injected into powerful enough recipients," Albert reminded me.

I cringed, remembering how a single dose given to a single, not yet fully developed weredragon had taken out half of a city block and killed a few thousand people, and then my brain stuttered.

"Albert, dragons and weredragons are some of the most dark matter heavy beings in any of the realms, right?"

"Yes."

He was already getting out the small vial of Anti-Technetium Serum (we'd decided to call it ATS for short during our brief planning session) that he'd been given "just in case" when we'd sent him off to track down Dryer, and was prepping it to apply to the vials of Technetium that sat in the small wooden crate in front of us.

"So, how is it that when they set off the weredragon in Sucre they didn't wind up taking out the entire city and a good chuck of the rest of Bolivia?" I asked.

Albert blinked, his hands halfway to the crate in front of him.

"It was a young weredragon. It wouldn't have had the reserves to cause an explosion much larger than—"

"Would it have reserves bigger than Trev's?" I asked, lacking patience for the long calm explanation that Albert seemed determined to give.

"I would imagine they would be similar, although your brother is a bit of a special case and has been training to access even more dark matter than—"

"MOME seemed to think that blowing up Trev would take out the entire city of La Paz, or more. Why wouldn't a young weredragon do similar damage? Or, at least HALF the city, instead of half a city block?"

"I don't know, Vic. Are you saying you wish they'd done more damage?"

I ignored the annoyed edge to Albert's voice and pushed on.

"No, Albert, I'm saying that maybe they didn't inject the other weredragon they took. They must have switched her out for someone else. They could have used some kind of illusion to make whoever it was look like the weredragon they took, so when we only found Siara and one other, we thought we had rescued everyone. So, where is the other weredragon?"

"Vic, we don't have time for this. The strike force is going to take this place out in a matter of minutes, and we have work to do."

I sighed, thinking about how Cronk and Sylvestra had been lured here and held captive in the dungeons, told they'd be forced to join the "right side," and how that explosion in Sucre hadn't been large enough to match the firepower that Albert, Siara, and everyone else had been predicting, based on how much dark matter a dragon had. Then I thought about the kind of person Rebecca Dryer was, or had been till a minute ago, and I thought about how the tunnel that led to this door kept going down and down, but didn't have any more torches on the wall. And a memory of the message my parents had left us with an abandoned boat niggled at the back of my mind.

"Damn it," I muttered. "Here, Albert, take my ATS supply. This should be more than enough to get you through this box."

"Vic, what are you doing?" he asked, even as he took the serum from me.

"We're about to level this place to the ground, and I can't live with the idea that there might be more innocent people trapped in here."

Albert stared at me for a long moment before saying, "Be careful." He nodded slowly, as though the action troubled him, and then handed me back one of the four serum vials I'd given him. "Between the two of us, we have extra, and you might need this down there. Good luck. I'll try to get out of here fast enough to tell them not to blow you up."

"I appreciate that, Al."

I winked, and Albert's eyes teared up a bit, and then I was turning and running out the door, hurdling over the lifeless body of Rebecca Dryer, swallowing the bile and guilt that rose in my throat, and hoping beyond hope that I wasn't about to get myself killed for no reason.

I T HAD BEEN a few weeks since I had run for longer than it took to escape a deadly situation, and even though running is usually a favorite activity of mine, I wasn't used to running with a bullet in my shoulder. It officially sucked. I doubted I would have managed it at all without the benefits of recently getting busy with a succubus suffusing my…everything. I'd briefly glanced at the wound after I'd started jogging and it had painfully and emphatically reminded me of its presence. The bullet appeared to have passed all the way through my shoulder. I had no idea if that was a good thing or not, but I was definitely worried about blood loss. Or I would have been, except that the wound was barely bleeding at all now and I didn't even feel faint. So, yeah, I was gonna have to give Azrael one hell of a high five later, because succubus power exchange seemed to be like gaining multiple superpowers at once, one of which was speedy healing or some shit.

Even still, the damned thing throbbed with every step, and I rather desperately wished I could shift into my snow leopard form to make the whole trip pass more quickly.

"Stupid dark matter dampening rocks," I muttered, as I ran deeper and deeper into the ever-darkening dungeon.

I was left to enjoy the dank dungeon air in my human lungs, and try to ignore the smell of decay that seemed to only grow stronger as I hurried down the dark, rough stone corridor, occasionally splashing myself with enough water that I wondered if this tunnel ultimately led to a pool or underground river, rather than the missing were-dragon I was hoping to find.

The puddles became more and more frequent, and I was more and more convinced that I must have passed through a doorway to an alternate realm at some point, because since when is there this much water in the middle of the Arizona desert? But alternate realm or not, the steep tunnel floor was getting more and more slick, and I would have fallen multiple times as I descended if a faint light hadn't started to flicker up ahead, reflecting off of the various puddles that streamed across the stone, thus warning me to watch each step as I wended my way farther and farther below ground.

By the time I'd reached the source of the light, I'd had to slow to barely more than a jog. Trying to make as little noise as possible, all while keeping my footing and not landing my ass in a puddle, was taking most of my attention, despite the clock I was racing to try to keep myself, and everyone else who might be down here, from being incinerated by the dragon strike force that was supposed to follow up on our Technetium neutralization run. So, yeah, I was more than a little tense as I rounded the last curve of the tunnel.

Which was about when I heard voices, and my legs slowed to an extremely cautious walk.

Between the pounding of my heart, the sounds of my own breathing, and the constant drip that had accompanied me for the past half kilometer or so into the tunnel—which had lately surged into the sound of steadily running water—I couldn't understand any of what was being said.

Someone was shouting, and many people were... moving.

A series of boulders strewn haphazardly around the area where the tunnel ended and something else began muffled the sounds from the other side, in addition to blocking my view. The burble of running water that had followed me for the past few minutes suddenly materialized in the form of a splashing creek. It must have been flowing underneath the tunnel I'd descended, but now it emerged to tumble over rocks and sand, running around the larger boulders that obscured my view. I had to hope its rushing would be enough to cover the sounds of my approach from whatever was on the other side.

I absently wished again for my snow leopard form, and even tried to call on it—my human feet could never match its padded paws for stealth and agility—but my attempts brought me the same nothing they'd gotten me the whole way down here. *Fuck this rock.*

For now, at least the boulders were lending me cover, as I tried to figure out what was going on beyond them. So there was that. *Thanks, rocks.*

This may sound like a stupid thing to say, but climbing with a bum shoulder is hard. Super-healing aside, my shoulder still throbbed every time I used my arm, and topping out an oddly shaped boulder to get a better look at the other side definitely counted as using my arm. On top of that, all the rocks leading up to the boulder were slick with water from the no-longer-underground creek, which made my feet slick when I finally reached the boulder I decided to scale. In other words, I felt more like an asthmatic whale floundering on the beach than anything else by the time I was able to see what was going on beyond the tunnel entrance.

So it was no wonder I nearly shit my pants when I heard a shout to my left. I was lucky I didn't just let go and immediately splash ass first into the creek, because I was certain I'd been spotted.

But the shout hadn't been directed at me. It had probably been directed at one of the hundred or more armed soldiers milling about in front of the giant underground lake that extended a few hundred meters ahead of me.

"**S**HIT, SHIT, SHIT," I whispered, as I dropped back behind the rock I'd been climbing and let my brain process what my eyes had just taken in. Over a hundred people, armed, marching in formation, apparently following shouted orders from a handful of MOME operatives wearing the same uniform I'd stolen earlier.

I took a deep breath filled with damp tunnel air and buried my head in my hands, trying to figure out how I was going to rescue these people, and… well, whether or not I should.

I mean, look, don't get me wrong, I'm not a fan of added casualties, but if everyone in this cavern was a MOME-trained soldier, did I really want to keep them from getting caught up in the dragon's strike force attack? Wouldn't that mean rescuing a bunch of people who were just going to try to kill me and my friends later?

I'd come here hoping to find the missing weredragon, who I suspected hadn't been turned into a weapon back in Sucre, but I wasn't even sure what I'd just seen. It had looked like an army. Was this the fighting force that Mom and Dad had tried to warn us about in their goodbye message? It sounded like an army, too… or did it? I took another deep breath, and did my best to listen over the sound of running water.

"Stop that!" shouted someone, followed by the unmistakeable sound of flesh hitting flesh. A shrill whistling sound pierced the air, then someone yelled, "Pick that up and try again. Don't test me. There's plenty of time to send you back to the vamps."

That… sounded a little weird.

I sighed, realizing I was going to have to sneak closer if I was going to figure out what was going on here, and I cringed, because every second I spent here was one second closer to getting torched by whatever the dragons had planned for the MOME facilities after we'd neutralized the Technetium inside them. Albert would probably be done soon, and as soon as he was clear of the building… hopefully he'd have time to tell General Aira I was in here before she lit the place up.

I couldn't think about that. One thing at a time.

The more I paid attention to the sounds on the other side of that rock, the more convinced I became that I wasn't listening to the training of a willing army. And I knew I would never let myself walk out of this place if even one person down here was an enemy to MOME. Hell, I even had second thoughts about leaving voluntary MOME employees behind.

I climbed back up to the top of the nearest boulder, grateful that my shoulder was starting to hurt less and less, careful to keep as close to the rock as I could, barely bringing my eyes high enough to see the spread of people below me.

Yes, lots of them were marching in formation and following orders, but… dotted throughout, especially in the group with the highest concentration of MOME guards spread out among them, there were… outbursts. The majority of the shouting, and all of the physical outbursts, were coming from that one group. A group in which the "recruits" kept dropping their weapons, sitting down in the middle of drills, and… attacking the MOME agents?

This shit was getting complicated, and I was running out of time. So I did the only thing I could think of. I dropped back down to the tunnel and prepared to swagger into the cavern looking like I had every right to be there.

Then a hand clamped across my mouth and I stifled a scream.

"**S**HHH… IT'S ME," whispered the hazy grey figure, turning me around after pinning me single-handedly to the boulder I had just descended, before I could even shift my weight to throw them.

I really hated how fast Renata could move sometimes.

"What the fuck are you doing here?!" I rage whispered, as soon as she removed her hand from my mouth.

"I believe you need help," she replied, in a much calmer whisper, as if that explained everything.

"Ok, but—"

"Ms. Marmot, can I be of assistance?" asked a deep voice that I hadn't expected to hear again anytime soon.

"Torrence?" I asked, looking up at the looming bovine who suddenly, impressively, appeared right behind Renata.

"Where the hells did you come from? Is there a party down here I wasn't aware of?"

Both Renata and Torrence blinked at me for a moment.

"A party would be inappropriate at thi—"

"No, I came from Hel—"

I held up my hands to forestall both explanations, throwing a glance over my shoulder and hoping that no one beyond the boulders had heard or seen the growing crowd out here.

"Yeah, yeah, yeah, sarcasm fail. I get it. Ok. Torrence, seriously, where did you come from? I had half assumed you were dead."

"I am not dead. Albert insisted on entering Dryer's office alone. I waited for him to return, then watched as Dryer dragged him into the dungeons, following from a distance."

"Wait. Does that mean you just watched us fight Dryer, without helping?"

"My assessment led me to believe that 'helping' would only end in one or more of us getting shot."

My mouth dropped open. I wanted to argue, especially since one of us *had been* shot, but he made a fair point. Dryer had been wandering around with the safety off on a gun pointed at Albert's head. Surprising her would likely have ended with Albert's brains decorating a wall.

"But you followed me down here without making yourself known because…?"

"I was following at a distance when I noticed the grey haze behind you. As I didn't know what it was, I thought it would be prudent to wait until the haze made itself known as friend or foe before I made anyone aware of my presence."

I did my best not to sigh, because we were making too much damned noise already.

"Which brings us back to the grey haze. Renata? Why *exactly* are you here again?"

"Hel sent me to follow you. Tracking you here was quite difficult, and I did not arrive until after the woman in the tunnel was dead. I assume that is the woman Torrence did not help you fight. I passed the cow man on the way down, but he did not seem threatening, so I left him alone. Hel did not say that I could not help you, but it was not clear at first that you needed help."

I stood there, waiting for more, but I should have known better. Renata just stood there blinking at me, as if she'd given all the explanation necessary for someone who had recently betrayed me, Azrael, and my parents to an out-of-realm deity.

Maybe she had. What did I know? Is there an etiquette for that? A certain number of days before you send flowers and a card that said, "Sorry I sold you out to the reigning monarch of the realm we met in," or something? Whatever. *So* not the time.

"Ok… well, we don't have time to sort through how weird it is that both of you are here right now, so I'm just gonna roll with it. Torrence, you said you owe me your life. Now might be a good time to pay that debt. To be clear, that does **NOT** mean that I want you to die— far from it. Renata… I'm still not sure I trust you, but whatever, if you were here to kill me I'd be dead already, so I'm going to have to assume you're cool for now."

I took a deep breath.

"We need to get close to the guards before they shoot us, so just… follow my lead."

I took a deep breath and steeled myself for the batshit thing I was about to do.

"Oh, and try not to kill anyone," I added, before I turned, grabbed my two accomplices, and stepped out from behind the boulder.

~~~

The first part of my plan worked. No one asked us questions until I'd dragged a subdued-looking
~~~

Torrence and a more solid-seeming than usual Renata right up close to the nearest set of **MOME** guards. They were still far enough away that we had a decent chance to get a look at the cavern that surrounded us. The air still smelled of damp rock and stale air, and the underground lake that extended from the back of the cavern went on farther than I could see. The "troops," such as they were, responded to barked commands, attempting to drill with **AR-15s** and basic marching patterns. They all practiced on the hundred or so meters of "beach" that stretched from where we'd entered the cavern to where the lake began. For every group of 25 "soldiers" (if soldiers was the word for folks who repeatedly ignored commands and periodically attacked their leadership) there were three **MOME** guards dressed just like the one I'd knocked out earlier.

The nearest three guards were milling about in the center of a group of grunts who were repeating a basic marching drill for—judging by their vacant expressions—the thousandth time.

"Where's Amy?" asked the first guard I nodded to, thus utterly ruining the rest of my absolutely piece of shit plan with a single question.

"Lying unconscious in the tunnel where I left her when I took her uniform?" I replied, before my brain could stop me.

You could say I panicked a little bit.

To be fair, this plan had never been much of a plan, and everyone but me seemed to have a gun, so I was kind of shitting my pants (only metaphorically for the moment, but possibly literally if someone pointed an AR-15 in my direction).

In defense of my not-actually-a-plan, it's worth noting that dudeface was probably expecting me to say "getting coffee while I process these yahoos," or something similar. After all, even MOME assholes tend to be maze rats just showing up to work every day. No one really expects a security breach, and even if they do, they don't expect the classic "I'm-Harrison-Ford-and-I-just-stole-this-uniform-what-now-punk" approach to security breaches. Which… might explain why the dude who'd just asked about Amy exhibited full-on, cartoon-level surprise when I punched him in the mouth and took his rifle from him. (Not sure why the guards all had bolt action rifles, while the training troops held AR-15s, but hey, it wasn't the first time I'd thought MOME was a bunch of idiots, so I didn't think much of it.)

Of course, stealing the gun would do little to keep the other guards from turning on me and opening fire with their own weapons, which is why I grabbed Where's-Amy as he was still reeling from the sudden punch to the face and pulled him in front of me as a human shield, making use of a really fabulous headlock I'd learned from my Krav Maga instructor a few years ago that left one arm free for gun wielding.

It was also why I'd brought friends.

Before the nearest guard could do more than jump back in response to me decking Where's-Amy, Renata had dropped them to the ground. I hoped she'd remembered the bit I'd added about not killing folks, but now wasn't the time to worry about it. Torrence, meanwhile, had the third guard in a very painful but non-damaging looking arm lock, and was dangling the woman's gun in one hand like a dirty set of underwear.

"Right," I said, looking around. "That could have been worse."

"Hey!" called someone from one of the other platoons. "Why do you have Gerald in a headlock and—"

The voice cut off abruptly, and a quick scan of the immediate vicinity suggested that Renata might be the cause, as she was no longer anywhere near us.

"Nice," I muttered, turning to see if any of the other guards had noticed what we were up to. "This might actually work."

Then a high-pitched whistling noise rent the air, and a cold shiver went down my spine.

"Troops, attack the intruders!" someone in the distance yelled.

Then over a hundred people holding AR-15s suddenly turned on us as one.

"**O**H. FUCK."

My mouth didn't have time to drop open in shock, because I was too busy swinging Gerald around to block any potential gunfire while Torrence dropped into a fighting stance immediately behind me. I would have to do the whole shock thing later.

I noticed the guard Torrence had been holding lying suspiciously still on the ground in front of him. I had to hope he was heeding the whole "don't kill anyone" suggestion and simply rendering them unconscious, but, again, no time to check. 'Cause we were being rushed by everyone in our immediate vicinity.

The nearest of the trainees lurched towards me in an almost mechanical motion, and I wondered if androids were a thing in the magical world that I had yet to learn about. The woman looked human enough, but if I'd learned a single damned thing in the past three weeks, it was that that meant less than nothing. At any rate, I was trying to focus on how she moved, not what she was, because she was clearly going to be the first person to reach me.

I was doing my best to position the still-struggling Gerald in between me and her, assuming that she would raise her gun as soon as possible and open fire the moment Gerald wasn't in the way.

I was giving her entirely too much credit.

Maybe because I expected her to fight like someone with free will.

Maybe because I didn't realize that her gun was made of solid plastic, rather than the multiple moving pieces that are supposed to make guns work. Something that became entirely too clear when she raised the gun up over her shoulder and tried to clock me in the head with it, instead of firing any bullets. Thankfully, I was able to duck, and get my not-Gerald-holding arm up in time to block the strike.

Which hurt like a baseball bat, since solid plastic training weapons don't skimp around on the heft. I was lucky it didn't break my arm. I had to drop the rifle that I'd stolen from Gerald in order to make the block, which was less than ideal, but I wasn't super stoked on the idea of shooting anyone, now that I knew the guns the grunts had weren't real. But it meant that I had to hold on extra tight to Gerald, because I didn't want him getting ahold of his rifle again.

Since he was still struggling with every move I made, I was contemplating switching to a choke hold until he passed out, but I didn't have time. The lady who'd nearly broken my arm hadn't decided to stop, just because it hadn't worked the first time.

I watched her hips and shoulders, waiting for her core to telegraph where her next move would come from, but I didn't have to bother. Whatever they were training these folks in, it wasn't hand to hand. She just lifted the fake gun up in her hands and brought it back down again in a hacking motion. This time I turned Gerald into it, letting his side take the hit as I pushed back into Torrence, who seemed to be using the first person who had approached him as a broom, swinging them so that they took out the legs of everyone else who came at him. I didn't have time to be impressed, but I made a mental note for later.

Meanwhile, the other twenty people who had been approaching behind the first woman finally caught up. And, since this wasn't a movie, they all decided to attack at the same time.

Thank Gwen it was the most uncoordinated attack I'd ever witnessed. Half of them tripped over each other, falling in a sprawl that blocked everyone behind them from making it to me. Which still left me fighting a half dozen people at once, but… they were awful. I mean, they moved with almost zombie movie jerkiness, and tele-graphed every move as if they were holding up signs saying "kick," "punch," "stomp." I was beginning to think that I was trapped in an old school Batman comic.

I smiled as I managed to block a few kicks with Gerald's legs, and then use him to sweep the legs of two of my nearest opponents who hadn't already tripped themselves. But any humor I might have felt at my opponents' lack of skill faded as I realized that the people attacking me were still managing to injure themselves, and they were eventually going to overwhelm us in enough numbers to also hurt me, Gerald, and probably even Torrence.

Ok, that last one might be a long shot. Tor-rence—likes to frolic in flowers and make daisy crowns in his free time Torrence—appeared to be a seventh degree blackbelt in every martial art I'd ever heard of, and a few I hadn't. He was taking down swaths of oncoming opponents, and barely working up a sweat. He took down incoming attackers almost as efficiently as Renata had dispatched the harpies in Hel's realm, but he didn't appear to be shifting between dimensions or anything, as far as I could tell.

Even still, the initial wave he'd been dealing with was apparently just the tip of the grunt troop iceberg, because the next wave of people attacking was so thick I could no longer see the lake behind them, or the entrance to the cave we'd come through, or anything but the wall of people that surrounded us. And even though they tripped over each other, and even trampled each other to get to us, we were *so* not going to make it out of here in one piece if they all came at us at once.

Plus, they were probably killing the people on the bottom of the pile, and that was kind of the opposite of what I'd come down here for.

"Gwendamnit," I muttered, as the crowd surged closer.

"What am I damning?" asked a familiar voice, from behind me.

I didn't look, because I didn't have time. I also didn't need to look to know Gwen was now standing behind me.

"Thissss issss a troublessssome ssssituation, Living Cat," Rhelia's voice commented behind me.

I was too busy dodging the three different training guns that were being bludgeoned in my general direction to express my utter astonishment that Rhelia was here too. I finally had mercy on Gerald, who'd been clocked in the head by one of the last attacks anyway, and was now hanging limply in my arms, and launched him into the closest attackers, hoping they would ignore him, since he hadn't been one of the "intruders" they were ordered to attack.

"You will need the whisssstle," Rhelia said from behind me. Her voice sounded mildly strained, and I had to assume that meant she'd joined in the fight.

"Do I even want to know how and why you're here?" I asked.

"Thissss wassss my ssssecond guessss for where MOME wassss ssssstowing their newesssst army."

That sentence held so many layers of implications, I didn't even know where to start, and besides, I had to keep fending off the wall of limbs and torsos encroaching on my space.

"Is this the whistle in question?" asked Renata's gritty voice, from somewhere close by. I was too busy grabbing my nearest attacker and pushing them back into the oncoming throng to notice.

"Perfect. Thank you," Rhelia said, before a high pitched trill cut through the air around us.

"Cssseasssse fighting," Rhelia called loudly, after the whistle cut through the crowd.

To my relief, and horrified fascination, everyone around us came to a grinding and eerie halt at the exact same moment.

"**N**ow, ssssleep," Rhelia called. I almost threw up when the whole crowd collapsed to the floor as one.

"That's going to give me nightmares," I muttered.

"It will be nice to have a bit of variety, won't it?" asked Gwen, from behind me.

"What would you know about my nightmares?" I asked, before I could think better of it.

"Goddess, remember? Besides, I was briefly your narrator, remember?"

"Thought you didn't have access to that info anymore?" I asked, turning to glare at her, despite myself. It was amusing to find Torrence staring bewilderedly at the red-haired goddess, even though they'd met before. Or maybe he was more surprised to see Rhelia here, seemingly having popped in out of nowhere.

"That doesn't mean I don't remember the few pieces I had to narrate already," said Gwen.

"Would you two sssstop bickering pleasssse? We have more presssssing issssuessss."

"Are the dragons still planning to raze this place?" I asked Rhelia.

"Yessss. Though General Aira agreed to wait until we emerged, before beginning the desssstruction."

"Well, at least she knows we're here. So…" I took a deep breath and looked around the cavern that was now the (hopefully temporary) resting place for around a hundred and fifty people. Renata was a grey haze in my peripheral vision, and looking around the room I had to assume that she was the one responsible for taking out all of the MOME guards. I didn't think the whistle had worked on them. "We still have to figure out a way to get all hundred and whatever people out of here, don't we?"

"Unlessss you wish to ssssacrificssse them for the greater good, yessss."

"Could have saved myself the detour, if sacrificing them had ever been the plan," I replied.

"I know we don't really have time, but seriously, how did you know to come down here?"

Rhelia sighed, "You sssstill know very little about what I wassss doing when MOME captured me in Bolivia. Did you never wonder what missssion I might have had that would have enabled MOME to detain me?"

I shrugged.

"Seriously, MOME has captured, detained, or killed so many people close to me that I honestly just assumed it was because you were a part-time dragon."

Rhelia laughed, but the mirth didn't reach her eyes.

"That issss cssssertainly the reassssson they put on paper. However, them catching me sssssearching their dungeonssss for ssssecret training facsssss-ilitiessss may alsssso have been a factor."

Right. Ok. Sure. I'd known Rhelia worked for the dragon realm's intelligence gathering. I was just... way behind on a few pertinent details about her work.

"So... you eventually realized they weren't in the Andean office, and then?"

"My nexsssst besssst guesssss wasssss Shanghai," Rhelia added calmly.

"But when they didn't have training facilities, you realized it was here instead, and asked Gwen to drop you off?" I guessed.

"Oh, they had the facssssilitiessss, they were merely empt—"

"There is something wrong with your redhaired friend, Victoria."

That was Torrence, whose shoulder appeared to be the only thing keeping Gwen off of the floor. To say that Gwen was looking unwell would be the understatement of the year, but I didn't know how else to describe it. Her skin was dripping sweat and had taken on an unpleasant yellow tinge. Her hair, normally a mane of fiery curls, now clung limply to her face and shoulders, and looked brittle enough to snap if I so much as breathed on it too hard. Not to mention, her legs didn't look like they were holding her weight at all.

"Gwen?" I asked, unable to formulate a more specific question.

"M'fine," she mumbled. "Jus'need t'get out've here."

Then she collapsed entirely, or would have, if I hadn't reached forward to grab her. Torrence looked as though he would have grabbed her in the next second, but I happened to be standing in the direction she collapsed, so catching her was all but required.

"Living Cat?" Rhelia asked, sounding startled.

"Gwen's sick or something," I muttered. After a few moments of shifting my balance, I managed to lever Gwen up onto my shoulder. She didn't weigh nearly as much as she should have; lifting her felt like lifting a small child. I suspected that was a bad thing. She already looked like a patient in palliative care.

When I finally reached a standing position, with Gwen draped over my shoulder in a fireman's carry, I found Rhelia and Torrence frowning at us.

"She is a creature of dark matter, so this dungeon is probably killing her," Rhelia said, her accent dropping away. I really wanted to ask her about when she chose to keep it and let it go, but now was definitely not the time.

"How could she have gotten here, with all the dark matter suppression going on?"

"She likely had a single chance to bring us here, and was then stuck. For someone as powerful as she, the getting here was perhaps not that difficult, but she would be even less capable of leaving than the rest of us, as the dark matter suppressors restrain all that she is, not just her magic."

I let my jaw drop, as I considered why on Earth Gwen would have found that to be a worthwhile risk. I couldn't imagine getting Rhelia here as backup was worth it, but maybe I underestimated how screwed we'd been before she mentioned the whole whistle business.

Which reminded me that I hadn't seen Renata recently, and just as I opened my mouth to voice the question, she stepped out of the shadows and stood beside us.

"It should be easy enough to lead the mind control victims out of here, but I am unsure of what to do with the MOME guards."

We all simply stood and stared at each other for a moment.

"I may be good, but I cannot convey all of these unconscious individuals to safety alone before the dragons would destroy us all."

"It's true," Rhelia agreed. "Even if we were to emerge and inform General Aira that she must wait a few hours while we remove innocents, I doubt she would hold her attack. She… is not fond enough of non-dragons to risk the delay."

"Right," I said. "Rhelia, how does the whistle thing work, exactly? Can anyone give directions, or just the whistle blower?"

"There is no magic to it, else it would not work here. I believe the first person to give directions after the whistle blows will be heeded."

I nodded towards the whistle she held in her hand, and cleared my throat for a moment.

She blew the eerie signal that had blown twice already today, and I struggled to keep my stomach in check as all the eyes of the sleeping troops opened as one.

"Everyone, please wake up and make your way to the tunnel in a calm and orderly fashion, helping those around you who need it. If there is an unconscious person nearby, please work with the people near you to carry them. We must all exit this facility as quickly and safely as possible." I tried to use my best theater voice, hoping the acoustics of the cavern would help where my own vocal chords faltered.

A moment passed before, adding fuel to a lifetime of nightmares, almost everyone on the cavern floor rose as one, beginning to calmly progress to the tunnel behind us.

"So. Damned. Creepy," I muttered, before turning to follow them with Gwen on my shoulder.

IT WAS HARD not to feel a giddy sense of relief as I led the march of over a hundred captives out of the heart of MOME's North American dungeons and up towards light, air, and freedom. I was leading the pack, because I felt guilty allowing anyone else to risk encountering MOME resistance on the way out.

Luckily, all the MOME mind control victims seemed to be more inclined to follow a leader rather than push ahead, which meant that the glacial pace I was keeping, thanks to having an unconscious goddess slung over my shoulder, wasn't pissing off anyone behind me. Still, about halfway up the tunnel leading back to the top of the dungeon, I passed Gwen off to Torrence, because I felt like my legs were about to give out, and the place where Rebecca Dryer's bullet had gone through my shoulder earlier was starting to feel like it was on fire. Also, with Rhelia and Renata engaged in a whispered conversation just a few meters away, and no guards showing up to be defeated, Torrence looked desperate to have something to do. When I asked if he'd mind carrying the unconscious goddess, he practically jumped with glee.

As soon as Gwen was draped over Torrence's shoulders, Rhelia pulled away from her conversation with Renata and dropped back to keep pace with him.

With zero fanfare, Renata appeared beside me.

"You must be careful with them," she said, coming slightly more into focus through the shifting haze that always seemed to surround her.

I could guess who "they" were, since there was an army of zombielike people still trundling along behind us, but as for being careful…that could mean about a hundred different things at this point, and chances were good I didn't even know what most of them were.

"What do you mean?"

"They are all still under a compulsion placed by the vampires. If we encounter anyone who—"

"Wait, *vampires*?"

"Yes. How else did you suppose they were managing mind control?"

"But I thought vampire mind control only worked on non-magical folks."

"Normally, that is correct. However, it seems that MOME has discovered that even magical beings are vulnerable to vampire persuasion when their dark matter is suppressed."

"How does that work, though? Don't the vampires need their dark matter to use persuasion? And then, how does that do any good? I mean, then you have an army of people who can't leave the dark matter suppressing rocks, or whatever—"

"That is what the aquifer is for," Renata interrupted, perhaps growing impatient with my continued divergence from her initial message of caution. "The water that wells there suppresses dark matter as effectively as the rocks it has filtered through. Once ingested, it stays in the system for days. Long enough to move the victims to where a vampire could manipulate them. And long enough to be forced to fight after they'd been 'trained' sufficiently."

My stomach turned at the thought.

"They made everyone drink that stuff?"

"That is what both my and Rhelia's observations would suggest."

"Renata… what are you actually doing here? Did Hel seriously tell you to follow me all the way here?"

It was difficult to see through the haze, but I thought she might have shrugged.

"My father provided MOME with his services on more than one occasion, in his attempts to pursue me. I was… concerned about the legacy that would leave behind. Ever since you informed me of his demise, I have been wondering what wrongs of his it is possible for me to right. When Hel dismissed me and suggested that I could maintain my usefulness by seeing what you were up to, I thought perhaps I could… what is the term, murder two birds together?"

I swallowed, unsure whether or not she was joking.

"Close enough," I admitted. " So, you're telling me that Edik had something to do with the MOME brainwashing scheme we're now up to our ears in?"

Renata met the question with silence, but the look on her face was answer enough.

"Great. Edik is still fucking with me, even from the dead."

"We are nearing the surface," Renata continued, ignoring my jibe at her dead father. I looked around the tunnels and realized that she was right. We'd almost made it to the top of the dungeons. Soon we'd be out of the dark matter suppressing rock.

"You must understand that the vampire charms holding these people will not break simply because we leave the dungeons behind us. They will be in danger of falling under MOME control again, should we meet anyone that has one of those whistles."

"Right. Got it. Dewhistle the whistle holders ASAP."

I glanced at Renata and decided she wasn't done.

"Anything else?" I asked, warily.

"It will take them days to break free of the compulsions, and they will need help to break them. Until then… they may need assistance getting through their daily needs."

I stared at her for a moment.

"Are you telling me I have to babysit a hundred zombie people so they can all eat, sleep, and shit properly?"

Renata shrugged.

"You do not have to, but if someone does not… it may be unpleasant for them."

Ugh. I did *not* want to be in charge of these people's wellbeing until MOME's hooks were out of them, but leaving them to the side effects of MOME's latest shitty plans to take over the world was unacceptable.

"Why did they even *want* a zombie horde? It's not like they could use their magic, with their dark matter suppressed. They would just be cannon fodder."

Renata's mist-shrouded form merely stared at me for a moment, while I wondered what I had said that was so stupid. Then it hit me.

"Gwendamnit. That was the whole point, wasn't it? Horrifying cannon fodder created out of our own allies."

Renata only nodded, mutely.

"Ugh… and by the time we figured out we were killing people who weren't voluntarily fighting for MOME, it would be far too late."

I had kinda felt like throwing up ever since I'd encountered the whole mind control thing in the cavern, but now I could feel the bile rising in the back of my throat. I swallowed, because I hated vomiting in general, and right now I thought it would be exceedingly inconvenient—even though the idea of leaving vomit on MOME property was kind of appealing. Then again, so was lighting the whole place on fire. And, since that was part of the ACTUAL plan, I decided to save my petty bodily fluid revenge, and work on getting all these innocent people out of the way so that a few dozen dragons could torch MOME's North American headquarters as originally discussed.

If only it had been that simple.

AS SOON AS we hit the top of the dungeon, the place where the dark matter suppressing stone ended and the normal prison began, Gwen seemed to regain her full weight. At least, that was my best guess as to why Torrence had suddenly collapsed under the unconscious redhead.

A guess that was confirmed when Torrence muttered, "How can *anyone* be that heavy?"

Considering that Torrence was nearly seven feet of pure muscle, that seemed like an odd question, but when I hustled over to grab one of Gwen's still limp arms to try to help pull her off the giant man-bull, I could see what he meant.

"Holy shit," I said, dropping Gwen's arm. "Could this be some kind of MOME trap?" I asked, looking between Rhelia and Renata, who had hustled over to check on the trapped tauren with me.

The four of us were the only people out of our entourage who were actually looking at anything. Everyone else seemed to be staring blankly into space, after shuffling to a halt behind us. I shuddered, trying to ignore the zombielike horde that had somehow become my responsibility until they recovered themselves. My eyes snapped to Rhelia's, since Renata's were half hidden in the "mist" that seemed to constantly shroud her.

"I do not think sssso. I think thissss may be how much sssshe normally weighssss."

"She feels like she's cemented into the floor, Rhelia. How can she walk, if that's how much she normally weighs?"

"She's a goddess, isn't she?" Renata asked. "That means she is *mostly* dark matter. Rather the reverse of the rest of us; we are blood and flesh that contain some dark matter, she is dark matter that has been molded to appear as blood and flesh."

"It would exssssplain why sssshe weighed nearly nothing when we were in the dark matter ssssupresssssing partssss of thissss facssssility. It issss likely that sssshe can control how much sssshe weighssss when sssshe is conscioussss."

"So what the hells can we do to make her light enough to carry?" Torrence asked wheezily from the floor, even as he managed to push Gwen a few inches to one side. It wasn't quite enough to free him, but it was probably helping his breathing.

"Carry who?" asked a muffled voice, from atop the brown, furred chest she was currently pinning in place.

The four of us all stared at the still-unmoving redhead on the tile at our feet.

"Gwen?" I asked, unsure if I'd imagined the source of the voice.

"I'll be fine in a few minutes," the voice said. "Just leave me here for now. I'm afraid I won't be able to make myself lighter for a bit, but by the time I can do that, I should have no trouble walking on my own."

"Uh…" I looked between Torrence, Rhelia, and Renata again, hoping one of them would have some idea of how to respond to that. "Gwen, we're… kinda still in the middle of the MOME HQ in Phoenix. I'm not sure we should just leave you here."

"Oh, don't worry about me. There's really not much those asshats can do to me. In my current state, they can't move me back to the one part of the facility where'd they'd actually be able to harm me, and as soon as I can make myself light enough to walk, there won't be anything they can do to touch me."

She sounded completely casual, as though she were explaining why her cinnamon buns needed a little more time to rise before she could put them in the oven.

"You sure abou—"

"You really should be going, Vic. There is much to be done still, and not much time to do it in. The fates don't like to be kept waiting."

"The fates?"

"I'll tell you all about it later," she said, her voice now muffled by the tile flooring that her face was pressed against. Torrence had finally managed to slide her off of his chest and onto the floor. "If there is a later. There won't be, if you continue to linger here."

"Right. Cool. That's not ominous at all," I muttered.

"Go, Vic. Seriously. You need to go, or there won't be anything left to be sarcastic about."

I was never sure how seriously to take Gwen, because she'd first shown up in my life as a naked crazy woman claiming to be my narrator. But ever since she'd revealed she was a goddess, it was difficult not to feel like there was a certain gravitas to everything she said. And when she said twice in one conversation that there was a chance there wouldn't be a "later" if I didn't get my ass in gear, I was going to listen.

"Gwenspeed," I said over my shoulder, as the four of us turned and headed farther up and out of the **MOME** prison complex, our hundred shuffling mind control victims in tow.

"Cute," said the muffled voice from the floor. "I see what you did there."

I didn't hear if she said anything else, because I was too busy running towards the exits.

IT WASN'T THAT I didn't find it suspicious that we didn't run in to a single MOME operative on our exodus from the building, it was just that I was too busy trying to figure out what Gwen could have meant by suggesting that there wouldn't be a "later" if I didn't hurry up. I mean, I got that we had a lot to do before MOME was completely out of business in the "accidentally/on purpose gonna blow up the universe" department, but I had been under the impression that we'd had most of that sewn shut by the time I got into the dungeons and found the cases of Technetium that I'd needed to neutralize.

If everyone else had found the stores of Technetium they'd been looking for, then we should have been golden. Rhelia and I hadn't exactly had a chance to debrief, but when I'd asked about the cache of Technetium in Shanghai, she'd said she'd got it. If all our other agents had been as successful as Rhelia and I, we should be pretty much Technetium free by now… which is why what Gwen had said made me nervous. So nervous, that I didn't think much of the fact that we didn't run into any regular security or staff members as we ran through the halls of what had been a fully operational MOME facility not thirty minutes ago. Although, even if I had thought of it, I might have brushed it aside as Dryer having tipped everyone off to our whole "burn it with dragon fire" program when she realized we were there.

I certainly would not have guessed it meant we were about to be ambushed.

By what looked like the entirety of MOME's fighting forces from across the globe… led by a short, balding mage with a wand aimed right at my heart, the moment I stepped out of MOME's main entrance and into the way-too-fucking-hot-for-September Phoenix sun.

I had barely enough time to register the entirety of the force raised against us—over a thousand people arrayed around the paved parking lot that stretched outside the double set of glass doors we'd just plowed through, including clusters of folks wearing far more leather than was appropriate for the climate draped over parked cars, concrete barriers, and at least one tank, and a frontline of people holding actual AR-15s with an eerily familiar vacancy to their eyes—before I heard the word "fire" issue from the mouth of the short guy holding the wand.

And instantly felt myself tugged to my right, and into a grey lanscape where the world around me seemed to be separated by a thick veil of water, and everything but me and Renata moved in slow motion. I didn't have time to wonder what the fuck was going on—though a vague memory of Renata shuddering while talking about pulling people into her dimension came to mind—because, slow motion or not, the bullets that had started spraying towards me and the hundred or so stragglers I'd just pulled from MOME's brainwashing basement were still moving as fast as a ball thrown by a professional pitcher, and dodging them was the focus of my entire existence. The spells being slung were moving considerably slower than the bullets, but they were still rolling inevitably towards us, and as far as I knew, no one in our entourage was bulletproof. Or spellproof.

"I can't save all of you," Renata said, her voice sounding pained. "There isn't enough time."

And she was right. Unless she had a few more tricks that I hadn't seen yet, there was no way she could move fast enough to move us all out of the way of these bullets. And the people behind me, the brainwashed innocents who were still compelled by the command I'd given them to follow me, were still coming out the heavy glass doors, and would keep coming until I gave them a contradicting order that they could all hear. Which was never going to work with all the gunfire and shouting going on. Gunfire that had already torn a hole in my sleeve and the skin of my arm, as I tried to dodge a hail of tiny obstacles that were coming at me in the fastest game of dodgeball I'd ever played in my life. Renata was busy dodging as well. She hadn't let go of my hand yet, but I could already tell this was never going to work—we were going to have to dodge in different directions soon. She couldn't even save me. Not to mention Torrence and Rhelia, or all the nameless folks we'd just pulled from MOME's dungeons. Not without getting herself killed. She needed more time.

And then I remembered that we were free of the damned dark matter suppressing powers of MOME's dungeons, and I didn't have to try to solve this one with nothing but a stolen uniform,

my winning smile, and the apparently unsup-
pressable powers of a dhampir.

I also didn't have time to plan anything, so I did
the first thing that came to mind. I held tight to
Renata's hand, and reached through time and
space.

25

AND WE DIDN'T go anywhere. Not really. Because I hadn't reached through space all that much. Just a few feet to the side of where we'd been. Mostly I had reached through time. Not far, only thirty seconds into the past or so. Just long enough to turn and watch myself, Renata, and Rhelia come plowing towards the doors that would lead them out into the open, only they were plowing in a strange slow-mo, while Renata and I seemed to be the only ones moving at full speed. I guessed this was what she'd meant when she'd once told me that time in her dimension moved differently than it did in others. Our hands were still linked, and Renata immediately began pulling me towards our earlier selves, but I resisted.

"Wait," I whispered.

Thankfully we were still in her liminal space, and I didn't think anyone could see us. Certainly, when I glanced over my shoulder, the short bald guy who'd fired a spell right at my chest wasn't doing anything but watching the door with the kind of manic anticipation generally reserved for toddlers and serial killers.

"We have to warn ourselves," Renata hissed.

"No, we can't warn ourselves, or we wouldn't be here. We have to stop the folks who never made it out the door, and send them somewhere else."

I might have only been doing the time travel thing for less than a week, but I was already pretty clear on the fact that you couldn't really change the past, you could just nudge the future a little bit. Because when I finally had talked to Rhelia about it, it had been clear that at no point had she experienced a reality in which we hadn't been working together to save Trev. She had never died, no matter how much it had looked like it, felt like it, to me the first time I'd seen it. But if I hadn't gone back in time, we never would have had the plan to begin with. You couldn't change the past, but if you didn't time travel the past would have turned out differently. So, I already knew that we weren't here to warn past me, or past Renata, or even past Rhelia and Torrence, because damn it, they'd made it out the door, and we couldn't change who left the building before the shooting started, even if we tried.

I hadn't noticed who had made it out besides the four of us, honestly, so as soon as the doors opened, and past me came storming out in slow motion, I pulled Renata along, and the two of us slid past Renata from 30 seconds ago, past Rhelia, who Renata seemed to make a concerted effort to bump into, and past Torrence. Then we plowed into the hallway, where most of the horde of mind control victims were making their way towards the doors at a slow but determined plod.

A few of them had moved more quickly, and were already blasting out the doors, even as we reached the main group. There was nothing I could do about them now. If they were outside, they were beyond my sphere of influence. I had to help the folks standing in front of us, before it was too late to save them. Then we would go back and save Rhelia and the others. We had to. There was no way that Trev was going to forgive me for getting his girlfriend killed for real. He'd barely forgiven me for when it hadn't actually happened.

But first Renata whipped out the whistle, which I belatedly realized she must have stolen off of Rhelia as we walked past her, and she let go of my hand, so that she could blow the thing where everyone could hear it.

The hundred(ish) magical beings, which I now noticed included every kind of being, from trolls, to pixies, elves, human mages, human weres, and an assortment of other folks I had no name for, came to an abrupt halt.

"I need everyone to hold hands," I said, nodding my appreciation to Renata. I had kind of assumed that I could just give new orders to the mind controlees, but that probably wasn't how this worked. "Hug if you have to, but I need everyone connected right away."

I shuddered, as I heard the army behind us open fire. It wouldn't be long before bullets and spells started making their way through the heavy glass doors into MOME. I had to hope they'd been magically reinforced, or something, because other-wise we weren't even going to have time to get us out of here without casualties.

Luckily, the folks who'd had their minds altered still seemed inclined to listen to whistle-given com-mands, and within a few heartbeats of asking, we had a group of a hundred or more people of every variety, including all the folks who still had unconscious MOME guards draped over their shoulders, all holding onto one another. It could have been a Coke commercial—if we hadn't all been about to die in a haze of bullets and spells, that is.

"Hold on tight," I said, grabbing the arm of the nearest person, an orangish-toned elf, slightly taller than Nethia, but similar enough in appearance that I assumed he was from the same realm. His eyes were as blank as any of the others, so I didn't bother engaging him in conversation. Even asking someone's name when they were in this state felt like a violation. They couldn't resist any question I asked them, so I didn't want to ask them anything. I was going to stick to saving their lives if I could, and if they felt like telling me about themselves once they were better, that was their business.

As soon as I gripped the orange elf's arm, Renata slipped the whistle back into her pocket and grabbed onto my other hand.

"Here goes nothing," I said.

And pulled over a hundred people through time and space.

ND SUDDENLY, I felt so drained that if I hadn't been holding onto two other people, I would have collapsed to the… cactus and yucca strewn ground? That wasn't right.

"The fuck?" I asked groggily, blinking at the high desert sun shining through a cerulean sky, baking away at the pink-tinged ground as though it were mid-July instead of early September. Because the desert didn't really give a fuck about things like seasons. Or at least, not a piddly season like fall. It gave a little bit of a damn about winter, at this elevation, but September was just an excuse to have pretty sunsets, as far as the desert was concerned. That was fine. I got that. High deserts made sense to me in their own way. What I didn't get was why we were in the rocky scrubland that smelled faintly of mesquite and juniper, when I'd been aiming for a certain grove of pine trees surrounding a singular oak tree just outside of Flagstaff.

"You did it," Renata said, holding me up while looking at me quizzically. "You got them out."

I blinked some more, and saw that she was mostly right. I seemed to have brought us all away from MOME.

But I should have been able to shift us all back to the grove. It wasn't that far away, and this was a lot of people, sure, but I had moved way more people than this back in Bolivia. Of course, that had almost killed me, but this group was like a tenth the size. I should have been able to make it all the way there, and I shouldn't feel so damned drained.

"I was trying to take us to the Tree of Life," I said, absently, as I took stock of where we were. I had also been trying to take us five minutes into the past, to make sure that we would have enough time to get back to the fight as soon as the shooting started. Maybe that was what had drained me so quickly. It was a problem I was beginning to ignore, as I started to wonder what the fuck these folks were going to do out here in the middle of the desert without any mode of transportation.

Renata shrugged.

"They are clear of the hail of bullets that MOME wished them to die in, so I think we can call this a success."

"But they can't stay here. The desert is no joke. September may as well be the middle of summer here, and they don't have supplies. Even if they did have supplies, they can't—"

"They will be fine," Renata said. "At least until we can make it back to them."

"You don't understand how quickly dehydration and sunstroke can take out the unprepared."

Renata shrugged.

"They are much better off than they were. You took them from certain death to a plausibly distant one that we have a decent chance of rescuing them from, *after* we have rescued the others."

I sighed. She had a point. And I didn't have the energy to argue. In fact, I didn't have the energy to do much of anything.

I put out my hand, and was glad that Renata placed the whistle in it without even a question between us. I blew the pattern that I'd heard Rhelia and Renata use, then cleared my throat.

"Seek shelter from the sun, try to find water if you can. Don't drink anything stagnant, only the moving stuff. Take care of yourselves and each other. If you can use your magic at all, do it. We'll be back to find you as soon as we can."

Then I turned and grabbed Renata's hand, and once more reached through time and space.

AND PROMPTLY FELL right on my ass. Thankfully, I missed the two specimens of yucca and prickly pear that were hanging out nearby. Not so the tiny barrel cactus that was now mostly embedded in my right thigh, nor the pointy rock that had stabbed me in the left butt cheek.

"Ow," I said, mainly to vent my frustration. It didn't hurt *that* badly. If anything, it was a bit of a distraction from the still-throbbing bullet wounds in my shoulder and upper arm. As I stood up, both the barrel cactus and the rock released me. Barrel cacti were relatively friendly, as far as cacti went— the thorns were robust enough to hurt, but they mostly stayed in the cactus when I pulled away and stood up. It was a fact I was grateful for at that moment, since I really didn't have time to pull a bunch of cactus spines out of my ass.

"I can't shift," I said to Renata, who was looking at me as though I were an untrained dog whose behavior she couldn't begin to predict.

"Can you reach your magic at all, or did shifting so many people full of dark matter suppressant drain you entirely?" she asked, looking nonplussed. I wondered if she was calculating how long it would take her to run us back to Phoenix in the liminal space she occupied.

I started to reach for my snow leopard form, but then thought better of it. I didn't know how much energy I had, and couldn't be sure I'd have enough to shift again, but if we needed to get from here to Phoenix in a hurry, without me shifting us through space and time, there was really only one useful thing I could do.

Renata smiled, from far below me, as I spread my wings and lowered my neck enough for her to hop aboard. I didn't know exactly how long it would take to fly from here to Phoenix, but it couldn't be more than a few minutes, could it? It would have to be enough. I refused to think that we couldn't make it back in time to save Rhelia and the others.

There had to be some advantages to being a dragon, damn it.

Like getting to light up the asshat who had given the order to fire on a bunch of unarmed brain-washing victims.

~~~

Fun fact: apparently, if you are a dragon with a dhampir on your back, you can fucking *fly* in liminal space, and thus turn what should have been a ten minute flight into a thirty second one. Honestly, with a trip that short, it was almost as fast as using Gwen powers.

And it was WAY more satisfying to dive at the head of MOME's forces from a few thousand feet and release a spray of molten fire right in the bald fucker's face.

Go ahead, ask me how I know.

And look, I am not a fan of killing. It made me physically ill to shoot that one MOME jerk, and it had even made me feel awful to incinerate Edik's diamond cranium, honestly. But all evidence suggested that dragon-me was way less worried about violence in defense of one's friends, and bald-manic-mage-dude had just unleashed a haze of bullets on me, my new dhampir friend, the
~~~

tauren I was coming to think of as a battle buddy, at the very least, and my dragon sister-in-law, not to mention the hundred brainwashed MOME victims who he didn't know I'd been able to remove from the line of fire.

So, yeah, I wasn't feeling too guilty about roasting the dicktart.

He deserved it, and dragon-me let out a roar of vindictive rage and triumph when his body was immolated in dragon fire.

Unfortunately, having their leader incinerated didn't miraculously get the rest of the troops to immediately cease hostilities. It did, however, serve as enough of a distraction to get Renata on the ground without getting her riddled with bullets. She proceeded to weave through our reality and her own, picking up the dozen or so hapless mind control victims who had managed to follow us out of the door the first time, and had since been standing awkwardly in a hail of bullets. As far as I could tell, Renata and I had arrived almost immediately after we'd left, mainly judging by how few bullet holes were riddling the brainwashing victims we'd had to leave behind. Sadly, it was a number greater than zero, but not by much. Most of them were still on their feet. And now they were getting sucked out of my field of vision, one at a time, faster than I could keep up with.

I didn't see Rhelia anywhere, but I didn't actually search for very long, because I was no longer in Renata's liminal space, and therefore suddenly presented a very large stationary target. I was alerted to this fact by the hail of bullets that abruptly began raining down on me.

I needed to focus on saving my own ass for a minute.

~~~

Damn, I was learning a lot in this battle. For example, did you know that dragon hide is basically bulletproof? True story. The slugs raining down around me in the bright September sun simply bounced off, falling harmlessly to the ground. The few that bounced back towards the troops who had fired them at me seemed to ping against the shields that the mages had set up. Shields that my dragon eyes saw as a light glow encircling certain troops. Certain troops. But not all of them. And my dragon brain, for all that it was excited to wale on some enemies, was also a bit faster than my human brain, I guess, because it came to the conclusion that those unprotected
~~~

folks were very likely to be even more of our brain-washed MOME victims. Perhaps dragon me could actually smell that dark matter suppressing water in them, or perhaps part of me simply realized that the only folks not likely to have shields would be the folks who MOME thought were expendable. So I pulled up before I could accidentally torch any of the folks who were shieldless.

Then I learned that dragon hides are bulletproof, but they aren't completely spellproof. Many of the spells that the mages hiding behind shields slung at me bounced off as harmlessly as the bullets did. Many, but not all. Someone threw another one of those creepy-ass acid clouds outward and I barely dodged it (dragon memory in action is awesome, and it warned me that the acid cloud wouldn't just bounce away), but I was too focused on dodging the acid cloud to successfully dodge the barrage of spells that followed in its wake, and one of those spells was nasty, and stung like a cat on fire. I didn't even get a chance to see what spell it was, but luckily whatever it was had only grazed my tail, and while the pain was sharp, it didn't seem to be slowing me down. I roared off the pain and focused on a bit of retaliation.

Which led straight to the next fun fact of the day, namely that while many mage shields protect against bullets, you know what they don't protect against? DRAGON FIRE. Seems like nothing is dragon fire proof, at least insofar as my recent experiments had shown. Which probably explained why, after charring one tank full of vampires and mages, and a few of the mages hiding behind the front line of AR-15 wielding, shieldless mindcontrol victims, Rhelia swooped in to nudge me away from the enemy.

I was pissy about it at first. Dragon-me still wasn't done wreaking havoc on MOME's troops, but Rhelia pushed and pushed with her iridescent ebon muzzle, and once I backed up far enough it was clear what the problem was. The dragon fire I'd unleashed on the tank was... well, it was spreading, quickly. And nothing the mages and vampires were doing seemed to be able to stop it.

Well, shit.

I mean, don't get me wrong, decimating MOME's ranks with dragon fire seemed like a fine idea. Right up until I remembered that those same mages, vamps, and probably weres, were highly unlikely to do anything to stop the fire from consuming the same mind control victims that I'd been trying to spare in the first place.

At least the conflagration that had once been a tank—and damn, I hadn't thought metal could burn like that, dragon fire was some seriously badass shit—was keeping most of MOME's front-line forces busy for the moment. But that wasn't going to stop the fire from taking out the mind controlled grunts, nor was it going to stop it from taking out most of Pheonix, if given enough time.

Ugh…I hate being an adult sometimes.

If it makessss you feel any better, Living Cat, you are sssstill a child by dragon sssstandardssss.

Then why am I here fighting bad guys instead of playing in someone's yard?

Rhelia made no reply, and it wouldn't have mattered if she did.

As I took in the flaming scene before me, I was tempted to try to remove all of the mind control grunts from the equation and just let MOME deal with the fire, but there were too many for me to remove them without getting a bunch of them killed, and MOME seemed to be having zero luck with the fire, despite having all but stopped fighting in order to put it out.

Right then—time to put the boost that getting busy with Az had given me to the test.

THE TANK THAT I'd originally torched had started setting off small explosions that lit up not just the MOME troops that surrounded it, but also the pavement it was on, and… everything it touched.

MOME had basically stopped fighting, though it wasn't entirely clear if that was in order to try to put out the fire I'd started, or because they only had a handful of people to try to kill left. Renata had removed all of the remaining mind control victims that we had led out, and now I couldn't see her in the fray. Had she taken Torrence with her? I couldn't see him at the moment either. Rhelia was certainly here, and a very large target, but no other dragons appeared to be present, and I didn't even know where Albert had wandered off to.

At any rate, it was handy that they were distracted. But less handy that they were trying to put out the fire by sacrificing mind control grunts carrying spelled blankets.

In fact, that ruined just about everything that was useful about the fire to begin with.

Which is how, seconds after I'd stopped spraying the very fire that had become such a threat, I found myself diving down through the smoke that now clogged the air above MOME's Phoenix HQ, shrieking, talons extended—because I feel like there's a certain expectation of fury with wings that needs to be upheld—towards the flaming wreck that had been a tank only a minute ago.

It was more flame than not, and with my quick descent I didn't have much time to assess where a safe place to grab it might be. Rhelia's warning about dragons not being immune to dragon flame was still fresh in my mind, but honestly, what choice did I have? MOME had decided to use the people they had unwavering control over to douse the flames, and they seemed to have given them some kind of spelled blankets to do it with, but that didn't change the fact that the flames were consuming the blankets almost as quickly as they were applied, and then leaping to the folks holding the blankets, with zero fanfare besides the screams of the victims.

So, yeah, I didn't have time to look around for the best place to put my talons.

There was something that looked like a small hatch open on the side of the vehicle, and while flames consumed every available surface around it, there didn't seem to be any flames inside of the hatch yet, so I aimed for that spot, hoping to grab the inside edge.

It would have been a different story if I'd had to carry the damned thing anywhere, but as it was, I just latched onto the inside edge of the damned thing and did my best to picture a familiar hell-scape where it would fit in nicely.

But nothing happened, and I could feel my scales begin to singe.

I let out a roar of frustration, and then saw the flap of feathered wings at my side.

Azrael? Where the hells did you come from? I asked, with far less irony than I should have.

But Az didn't say anything before they kissed me. And I had just about a half second to think of how weird it felt because I was still a *dragon*, so Az was basically just making out with a small portion of my lip, but damned if that didn't get my dragon blood going, and then bam, I felt the power transfer initiate. Apparently, there were a few perks to having *already* gotten busy with a succubus. And I didn't have time to question how any of that worked, because suddenly, still gripping the flaming tank that was now causing the skin beneath my scales to smolder, my power finished the reach I had tried to initiate a moment ago, and then I was in hell.

OTH LITERALLY AND figuratively, that is.
Because of course, with Az's help, and
considering how close we were to the
seam that ran near here, I'd pulled myself
into that damned canyon of dark matter suppression, complete with orange sky barely visible
between towering cliffs, purple sun, and air tinged
with sulphur.

Which was actually great, because it seemed to
be the only thing that could suppress the dragon
fire (and wasn't *that* interesting—did dragon fire
run on dark matter, then? It must, and that would
explain why it was so damned hard to put out, and
also why it would eat into dragons as well), but I
only had half a second to consider the implications
of all of that before my whole world narrowed to
one of excruciating pain.

I didn't think it was the naked red squirrel thing that was sitting on top of my chest causing the agony, but I couldn't really tell. I'd fallen to my ass as soon as I'd landed in this damned canyon, and I couldn't see much of what was going on.

I could see that the fire on the tank had been put out, which was great, and I had to assume it meant that no part of my body was currently on fire, but apparently turning human and having human nerve endings to experience the remnants of whatever burning I'd just experienced was the opposite of fun.

And then Azrael started screaming at me.

Maybe they were trying to reassure me. How were you supposed to tell what a red demon squirrel was saying when the translation magic didn't work and all you heard was the sound of a thousand tortured cats every time they opened their mouth?

All of which ceased to matter for a moment, as I passed out from the pain.

When I came to again, Az was staring into my face, looking concerned. I wondered how long I'd been out, but decided it couldn't be more than a minute or two, because everything was exactly as it had been before consciousness escaped me. Also, Az hadn't abandoned me yet.

"Are we really going to have to climb out of here to get back?" I asked Az.

Who looked at me as if I were a very slow child, for a moment.

I decided to lie down for a bit and let my brain catch up to reality.

Had we come through a seam? I had shifted us here, this time, but used the seam as a guide, because it made the whole thing more energy efficient. What about the last time? The last time I'd used the seam in the dungeon from MOME. Which, Sol had reminded me a few days ago, didn't require any special powers to do. Nons (muggles, normal humans, whatever you wanted to call them) occasionally stumbled through seams, right? So... that meant that I should be able to go back through the seam here. The first time I was brought here, I was dropped off by MOME, tied up, and had no idea how seams worked, so it hadn't occurred to me I could get back from here, besides, I would have just wound up back in the dungeon, so that wouldn't have helped me. But this time, I had no real reason to care about going through the MOME dungeon. Sure, it might slow me down, but not nearly as much as climbing the cliff would.

Part of me wanted to climb up just to check on Siara, but for one thing, I was still largely a ball of agony. For another thing, I still had a battle to fight, and even though it was tempting—so Gwen-damned tempting—to just lie down here and take a break for a minute because damned if I wasn't covered in burns, and just generally beat to shit, and felt like I deserved a break after saving everyone's asses from dragon fire…

Of course, I'd been the one to set the damned fire to begin with, and there were still people I loved back on Earth, possibly fighting MOME, and possibly in mortal danger, and if anything happened to one of them because I wasn't there to help, I—

I was suddenly on my feet, Az perched on my shoulder, doing their best not to gouge me with their little sharp-assed squirrel claws—which I sadly was in too much damned pain elsewhere to even feel, but bless their little squirrel heart for trying—and feeling around in the air for the edge to the seam.

"Here goes nothing," I said, hoping that this seam really did lead back to the MOME HQ in Phoenix and not to some other dimension where some other freaking monster was going to swallow me whole before I could even get my bearings.

D ID I SERIOUSLY jinx myself? I wondered, blankly, as I reached the front door of the MOME compound, only to grind to a halt in horror, my arms and ribs aching with the burns they'd received earlier. Had I *actually* come through the door to another dimension? I wasn't sure what I was seeing, but it was something out of a nightmare inspired by Cthulhu and an oyster having terrible messy sex and then producing... whatever this was.

"What the ever-loving hells is that?!" I asked Az, who was now standing beside me in their winged human form.

"Hmmm?"

Az sounded distracted.

"Az, what *is* that?" I repeated.

"That, Luv, is someone you would do best to avoid if you're able." Their voice was calm, but they were twitching in a way that was anything but. I couldn't say I blamed them.

I'd basically sprinted here after pushing through the seam in the dungeon, burns or no burns—and thanks to Az kissing me rather thoroughly, as soon as we'd made it out of the dark suppressing stone of the dungeons, the burns were barely noticeable anymore. I'd shifted to snow leopard form right after that, in order to move faster through MOME's sterile, fluorescent-lit interior design nightmare, and then I'd shifted to human as we'd reached the heavy glass doors, apparently for the sole purpose of interrogating Az about the hellscape that lay before us. Technically I supposed it was just the one hell-creature, and not a whole hellscape, but… clam shell, tentacles, giant fanged maw, lots of writhing, and dripping… it painted quite the scene.

And whatever it was, it was using suckered, dripping tentacles to grab… everything around it. As I watched in a sort of fascinated horror, it shoved everything into its maw, from people, to gear, to the one remaining tank. It was even grabbing up pieces of flaming pavement and choking them down.

And…

"Oh…" I muttered.

Az turned their silver gaze in my direction.

"What?"

"I still don't know what it is— your explanation was no help at all, BTW—but I think I know why it's here," I said, watching as the thing grabbed an AR-15 out of the hands of a human and swallowed it whole, followed immediately by another chunk of flaming concrete that some of the MOME mages had launched in the creature's general direction after managing to sever and lift it using some form of telekinesis.

"I think someone brought it in to do cleanup," I clarified.

I winced as it grabbed one of the mages that had been manipulating the section of flaming concrete, swallowing him down too.

Az stared at the thing again, and shuddered.

"I'm not sure that's an improvement on the fire, really," they said. "Thanatos does ingest dark matter in any form, but he's… not the most agreeable demon on most days, and… he rather despises being summoned against his will."

And yeah, I could kinda see that. The thing was eating things and people as indiscriminately as the dragon fire. But then something caught my eye that made me realize that whoever had brought it here had probably intended to kill two birds with one stone. My spine straightened in terror, though, as I realized that they were likely to kill a whole lot more than two birds.

"Shit, Az, we have to stop them," I said, pushing the doors open and deciding that I was going to have to brave the monster, no matter how pants-shittingly scary it was.

Az started to object, but then they must have seen what I did, and they were sprinting alongside me.

Someone was trying to sneak up on the creature with a syringe—filled with something that looked an awful lot like Technetium.

U GH. THAT THING, Cthulhu-Oyster hybrid, whatever the fuck—Thanatos, I guess Az had said—was huge. And the closer I got to it (shooting past Az on my much larger wings), the larger it seemed. Not just from the perspective change, but like it had actually grown since I'd started watching it. Maybe it had? After all, if what Az said was true, the damned thing consumed dark matter, and maybe that was the kind of thing that made a creature gain mass quickly? I mean, why the fuck not? Everything else about it was horrifying, so why not add getting visibly larger every time it ate to the list?

Racing towards it, even shifted to my dragon form, made my stomach feel like a solid cold lump of terror. I hoped that, as a dragon, I was too big for the creepy thing to swallow, but I was not particularly reassured. At any rate, I wasn't aiming for the damned creature. I was aiming for the idiot with the Technetium.

Because injecting Technetium into something that was basically a dark matter repository seemed like a terrible idea. Or just a really good way to kill everyone and everything in this whole city… and possibly the entire universe, as previously discussed.

And damn it, I knew that had been Dryer's master plan, but I didn't think the rest of her minions were so stuck on it that they would still be working towards it even after her death. I mean come on, who is *that* committed to taking out the whole universe? I mean, I'd even flambéed the short asshat who had seemed to be in charge of this whole regiment, so who was going around ordering people to blow up the world *now*?

But all of that would have to get filed under "shit to worry about when you're not about to die," because right here and now I had to worry about preventing the end of the world. Again.

And dude with the syringe knew how to hustle. He wasn't wearing any of the useless radiation gear that might slow him down and—

Shit.

I wound up slamming into both him and the clam-Cthulhu love-child demon, because fuck if he didn't reach the tentacled menace before I did. And not *one* of the damned tentacles even *tried* to grab him. Which could not be said for me. I was half-wrapped in one, even as I reached forward with my scaled snout—ignoring all the pain radiating out from my sides and forelegs, where I'd been burned—and tried to nudge the syringe-carrying fool out of the way. But the dude was moving with the kind of determination reserved for sprinters and zealots, and I could do little more than nudge him to the side, as the tentacle of the monster clam tried to pull me into its maw. So I slapped the monster clam with my tail, reaching my neck forward again to crash into the Technetium wielder, but I was too late. I watched in horrified silence as the syringe plunged into a waving tentacle.

I didn't even think, I just shifted with every Gwendamned thing I had.

And I caught just the briefest glimpse of an orange sky with purple sun, before blackness took it all away.

I BLINKED MYSELF awake to a purple sun in the orange sky, almost exactly where it had been the last time I was here.

"Gwendamn, I really need to get some tests done," I muttered, to no one. Or maybe to the small, electric blue rabbit that was sitting on my chest. It, unlike Az in squirrel form, had plenty of fur. It looked downy soft, was almost small enough to fit in my palm, and had eyes the size of nickels. It was practically an anime character.

"Hello there," I said. Since, you know, this was a hell realm, and the shrieking squirrel that I knew as Azrael was also a talking angel back on earth, so, this guy could be anyone. There was no reason to be rude.

"Hello, human/dragon female," the bunny replied, blinking mildly.

I tried to sit up, without really thinking about it, because, even after everything I'd been through, a talking blue bunny was a bit startling. Only I couldn't, because the damned thing felt like it weighed at least a hundred pounds.

"Oh, pardon me," the bunny said, hopping down beside me and causing a tremor in the earth. "Still digesting," it added, as though that explained why it weighed about a hundred times what it should have.

"Do, uh… do you know how long I was unconscious just now?" I asked, wondering if it would be rude to ask the bunny how the hell it spoke English aloud, when translation magic didn't work down here.

"From the moment we arrived here, until just now? Only handful of minutes, by your reckoning," the bunny said.

"Spent time in England?" I asked, wondering why all the demons I was meeting sounded like they'd spent time in the UK.

"Yes! Devonshire. One of my favorite haunts when I've been visiting your world. Although there are many other places I've enjoyed. Earth is a lovely world all around, but Devonshire was where I learned to speak English. I've always loved the accent, though of course I try not to emulate it—very difficult for some folks to understand."

Sure. Why not? And then my brain let go of the fact that the bunny had a British accent, and was producing spoken English from vocal chords that shouldn't have been able to manage those sounds, and focused on the fact that it had said "from the moment we arrived." We arrived. *We.* I was pretty sure that I had only been touching one thing when I'd shifted us here. I swallowed, but tried not to let my newfound fear of the tiny blue bunny show on my face.

"Did, uh… did anyone else show up with us?" I asked, blinking and trying to look around.

"The unpleasant fellow who stabbed me with a syringe arrived here with us, but he took off running immediately after we landed. Thank you for shifting us here, by the way. I don't think I would have been able to reach the seam before the Technetium took effect, and I rather prefer not becoming disassociated atoms."

I swallowed again, but this time the emotion I was trying to contain wasn't fear exactly, it was the overwhelming sense that the universe was just going to keep fucking with me until I died.

"Do I even want to know how you know about that?"

The small bunny twitched its nose as though it might be offended, so I tried to look apologetic.

"I mean, I know shit about shit when it comes to the magical world, and I really don't know who you are, so forgive me if this is something you're a well-known expert on, but I was under the impression that it wasn't widespread knowledge that Technetium reacted poorly with dark matter, and that MOME was weaponizing it."

"Hmph… perhaps it wasn't widespread knowledge before that little power play Dryer pulled in Sucre last week. But you can bet your hat that everyone whose existence relies on dark matter is talking about it now. Perhaps my people are more sensitive to the news than others might be, but you can be sure we started the process of changing our names as soon as we heard."

Which just left me blinking at the bunny, as my brain tried to put all of that together.

"My dear, I'm a demon; I can be summoned by anyone who knows my true name, and, if they've drawn a powerful enough circle, I can be held and made to do as they wish. Surely you've heard of this?"

"You mean outside of paranormal romance books and horror movies?" I asked, not sure what the bunny expected me to say. It blinked at me in a way that was decidedly unbunnylike. Then again, he was also a giant dark-matter-eating clam/squid of doom that could talk, and that shouldn't have been on the list of bunny-approved activities either.

"It might be worth mentioning that, until a few weeks ago, I didn't really know that magic was a thing," I added, just in case.

"Ah, well, I suppose I will have to forgive your ignorance, then, but suffice it to say that even those of my kind who had never visited Earth began the arduous task of legally altering their names here in the realms. Unfortunately, the process takes days, even under normal conditions, and every demon in the realm applying at once is hardly normal conditions. My own paperwork hasn't gone through yet, and some clown at MOME must have had a file on me, because the next thing I know, I'm being summoned into the midst of a battle where some heathen has unleashed dragon fire into the ranks and—"

I tried to cover up my rising embarrassment by interrupting.

"Do you have a way of purging the Technetium from your system?" I asked. "This canyon isn't the best place to hang out long term."

The bunny eyed me again as if I were slow, but then seemed to relent.

"I do not need to purge it. It will leave my system in due time, just as any other substance would. My body clears such things the way that your own clears alcohol, or any other toxin that doesn't kill you first."

"Oh?" I asked.

The blue bunny nodded.

"I don't mean to be indelicate, but the substance will pass through me with the rest of my food. I must say, I'm glad I was able to feast so nicely just before you brought me here, as it will, ah…. it will help move things along, if you take my meaning."

Right. Cool. The bunny-demon was going to poop out some Technetium in…however long it took bunny demons to digest such things.

Well, fine, that was actually awesome, because, yeah. I didn't want the bunny demon to die, just because of my hasty fire breathing in MOME's general direction.

"Look, it has been very educational meeting you, and thanks for not killing me earlier, but I need to head back to that damned battle."

I stood as I spoke, and the bunny nodded again.

"Thank you for your assistance, Miss…"

"Vic. You can call me Vic," I said.

"Indeed, Vic. It was a pleasure. Thank you for saving my life. I hope to see you again in better circumstances."

I laughed, and the bunny looked taken aback.

"Sorry. It's just that my life seems to be one disaster after another, lately. I would love to see *anyone* again in better circumstances."

"Ah, yes. Well, best of luck, and do keep an eye out for the one who summoned me."

"Who summoned you?" I asked, even as I felt around for the seam in front of me.

"If I knew the chap's name, I dare say I wouldn't have let him order me about. He'd never have had a chance to…" The bunny seemed to realize he was mumbling, but quickly refocused. "Tall gentleman, older, white beard, white hair, long nose."

"Shit," I breathed, just as I stepped through the seam and back into the dungeons at MOME.

As I RAN up the dank stone stairs, pulling in lungful after lungful of stale air laced with moss, old urine, and traces of even worse refuse, I desperately hoped that Albert hadn't betrayed us. After all, summoning a demon to clean up a mess of dragon fire wasn't necessarily an evil act. Thanatos had seemed all too happy to eat up a bunch of dark matter, and it had only seemed mildly ruffled at having to be emergency shifted to the demon realm to poop out some Technetium. So it wasn't unthinkable that Albert had summoned it, and then some MOME assholes had done their usual trick of ruining everything by trying to blow people up. That was just MOME being MOME, really.

But Blue Bunny had seemed pretty convinced that whoever had summoned him was someone to keep an eye on. That didn't bode well. Of course, it would be easy enough to mistake the jerk who summoned you from the hell realms as someone who worked for the corrupt government that was trying to kill everyone. Alternatively, it could be that there was another tall, white-bearded, white-haired mage summoning demons at this battle. I really hoped it was the latter. Because if Albert had somehow turned on us…

I didn't want to think about that one, and I didn't have time to, as I finally noticed that I'd already burst into the hideous, fluorescent-lit hallways of MOME's upper levels and was quickly sprinting towards the exit, somehow ignoring the burning aches that still permeated my arms and sides. I reached the glass doors that showed me the parking lot, and ground to a halt once more. I wasn't sure what I'd been expecting. As far as I knew, I'd only left a handful of allies behind to battle the remains of MOME's forces, but maybe something in me had somehow expected Renata, Torrence, Rhelia, and Az to miraculously overcome that whole force with just the four of them. Or maybe I'd just expected the reinforcements to arrive, and for the dragons to be kicking the ever-loving crap out of everyone else.

And maybe something like that had happened. There were more of my allies outside than I'd expected to find. A lot more, actually. I barely had time to register them all, but they ranged from the usual suspects—Seamus, Sol, Trev, Rhelia, Renata, Torrence, and Az—to folks I had never really expected to see again like Mr. Topaz and Ms. Rebuke from Flagstaff High, a surprisingly large portion of the Unterberg council, Sylvestra and Cronk, Seamus' Moms, Sol's Abuelita—accompanied by a half dozen giant panthers, and last but not least, my Mom and Dad.

Yet the tableau before me was anything but hopeful. For one thing, the sky above it wasn't full of raging dragons, and it really should have been by now, since we'd clearly gotten everyone out of the MOME building. Where the fuck was General Aira? For another thing, just outside the building, on the too-hot pavement baking in the September sun, surrounded by an absolutely still ring of mages, mind control victims, and the surreal roll call of all the people I had met in the past few weeks, stood Albert, with one arm wrapped rigidly around Trevor. All eyes were focused on the two of them, and filled with varying degrees of terror.

Their posture could easily have been mistaken for a casual one-armed hug, if it hadn't been for how limp Trev's form was, and how Albert's normally easygoing face was transformed by a severely locked jaw, and a wild gaze that looked anything but sane.

It was an expression I'd seen before somewhere, but I didn't have time to try to place it, because Albert was in the process of raising a syringe in his free hand, all while shouting something I couldn't hear through the quadruple-paned glass doors.

Until suddenly I could hear it—though I didn't have time to make out what it was—because I'd shifted myself outside, right in front of them, so close that my momentum carried me between them, almost knocking Trev out of Albert's grip, even as I felt the prick of a needle at the base of my neck.

I didn't wait for the tingling sensation that accompanies a liquid being injected into the bloodstream before I pulled on the seam that was becoming as familiar to me as the curtains in my old bedroom. And I didn't wait until I'd pulled that seam open by hand, either. I just pictured the one place that I knew could save me, made sure I had a firm hold on Trev, and shifted.

~~~

"Fuck. This is getting old," I muttered, as my legs decided they couldn't hold me up anymore. *At least*
~~~

I'm not fainting, I thought, as I sank to my knees. I was tempted to go all the way down; to let my head rest against the rocks and take in the orange sky with its purple sun, inhale a few lungfuls of disgusting sulphur-tinged air and relax for a minute, but a small part of my brain reminded me that now wasn't the time. I was going to have to enjoy the view and wonder why I kept ending up here some other time.

Trev had collapsed right along with me, not stopping at his knees as I had. Probably because he'd been unconscious before I'd even arrived on the scene. He was breathing normally, so I wasn't too concerned, for the moment.

Which is why I felt I had time to turn and look at the bastard I'd started to consider a friend, or at least an eccentric and somewhat flakey ally, and who was now shouting obscenities at me as though I'd killed one of his beloved pet iguanas and was wearing its skin as a hat.

"RUINED EVERYTHING. AGAIN!! WHY WON'T YOU JUST DIE, AS YOU'RE SUPPOSED TO!? THANATOS SHOULD HAVE DEVOURED YOU, ALONG WITH EVERYTHING ELSE! THE SEAM SHOULD BE RIPPED OPEN BY NOW! I SHOULD BE KNEE DEEP IN BODIES, WITH THE

INVASION IN FULL SWING!!! HOW DO YOU KEEP SURVIVING?!?"

With all the yelling getting shriller by the second, until it seemed that Albert might start to levitate by dint of sound waves alone, I probably shouldn't have been surprised when he launched himself at me, while I was still on my knees, crushing me into the dirt right next to where Trev had gone down. I probably should have been even less surprised that he started to try to strangle me and repeatedly bash my head into the ground. I say try because, well, regardless of what had possessed Albert to start acting like an angry teenager who'd never really learned how to fight, I was a teenager who *had* learned how to fight and, exhausted or not, I was not about to let someone mush my head into the dirt.

So I rolled out from Albert's trembling grasp and pinned him beneath me, slapping him, because part of me was really struggling with the whole "your mentor-type-person has betrayed you and lost their mind, maybe you should consider knocking them out" thing, and I thought maybe a few reminders of why he couldn't take me in hand to hand combat (which was his only option, since we were in everyone's favorite dark-matter-suppressing hell canyon) were in order.

"How do you do it?" Albert asked, after I'd slapped him a second time, then stood up to place myself between him and Trev. I didn't think there was much he could do to Trev in this place, but I also hadn't thought he would try to inject Trev with Technetium and wind up injecting me with it instead, so what the fuck did I know?

"How do I do what, Albert?"

"How do you survive? How do you keep refusing to die, no matter how many times you should be killed? How do you *always* manage to stop me from turning this abomination into the weapon he was meant to be?"

He gestured towards Trev as he said it, and a chill went down my spine as I watched him get up from the red dirt of the canyon floor. There was something *off* about the way he did it. It was clumsy, like he was drunk, or like everything about his body wasn't quite where he'd expected it to be.

I was distracted from assessing the movement, though, as a different movement caught my eye in the shadows behind Albert, a brief flash of blue—so quick I wasn't sure if I'd imagined it—in between the puddles of darkness.

I locked my eyes back onto Albert, now warier than ever.

"What do you mean, Albert? As far as I'm aware, this is the first time you've tried to blow Trev up. And I'm a little shocked that you decided to do it in person, since that would have killed *you*, along with everyone else in the greater Phoenix area, not to mention, you know, maybe the universe."

"Ha! You ridiculous human! Don't you know anything? Do you really think your precious *Albert* would try to harm you monsters? The bitch would adopt every magical misfit in the world given half a chance. 'Albert' isn't here, and can't stop me!"

Then whatever it was, which sure as fuck looked like Albert, but apparently wasn't, launched itself at me and resumed trying to strangle me, and for just a moment I was so startled that I let it.

"Did you really think a bullet would stop me, you pathetic, backwater mistake? I am the daughter of two of the most powerful mages to ever grace MOME's training grounds. I am the backbone of a centuries old organization meant to protect magical people from the idiocy of humans and the taint of mixed-breeds like you. I am more powerful than you can even imagine, and I. Will. End. You."

That last sentence was punctuated with the fervent shaking of my neck, which got old real fast, shock or no shock.

I brought my hands down in a move I'd practiced thousands of times over the years, forcing Albert's arms down and breaking the stranglehold. Then I headbutted him, with a silent apology to the real Albert as I heard the nose break.

"Damn it, Rebecca," I wheezed, as Albert's body stumbled back. "Don't hold back. Tell me how you really feel."

Rebecca Dryer, or whatever form of her was here looking like Albert, didn't reply, perhaps *finally* having learned the value of not monologuing in the middle of a fight. Instead she used Albert's body to charge me again.

And, look, Rebecca Dryer might have been a powerful mage—I wasn't sure how those things were measured, and I'd never had to fight her with magic, since she'd always sent other people to do her dirty work for her— but she sure as shit wasn't any good in a fight *without* her magic, and especially not in a borrowed body. I still had zero clue how she'd done it, and whatever it was, the fact that it still worked even with dark matter suppressed was terrifying. But she'd clearly managed to take over Albert's body sometime after he'd shot her. And yeah, three weeks ago that would have been mind-bogglingly creepy, but now it was basically just Thursday.

I had no trouble sweeping Albert's legs out from under him when Rebecca forced his body to charge me, but that left me in a predicament. I knew a ton of ways to put Albert down permanently, but I didn't want *Albert* to die—assuming that Rebecca forcing her spirit into his body hadn't killed him already, that is. I didn't really know how this worked, but I was pretty sure that fucking Albert up physically wasn't going to do much to Rebecca's spirit in any permanent sense. It would probably seriously mess up Albert, though. Which meant that Rebecca would be more than happy for me to fight him.

"Fuck," I muttered, hesitating to follow up my leg sweep with anything more damaging, while Rebecca got Albert's body to its feet and then grinned with a creeptastically manic facial expression.

"You've realized you don't want to hurt your precious mentor, haven't you?" she asked, sneering at me. "Well, you're about to lea—"

I never got to hear what I was about to learn, because Albert's body collapsed then, limp and lifeless, to the ground.

A large belch sounded from behind Albert, as a small blue fur ball hopped over his prone form.

"Thanatos?" I asked, unsure if I should be glad to see the tiny (in this realm) demon.

"I did not like that woman," Thanatos said in an aggrieved tone, "but she was very tasty."

"Uh… how did you… uhmmm, I mean, don't you usually eat dark matter?"

"Me? Oh certainly. I'd rather feast on the stuff. But there's no dark matter here in the canyon, you know."

"Ummm… yeah. I know that. The rock suppresses it."

"Indeed! Well, I was growing rather peckish, and this form isn't an ideal one for scaling cliffs to seek out food."

"Right… but what did you eat just now?" I wasn't 100% sure I wanted to know the answer, but I figured it might be important.

"Why, that mage's shadow, of course."

"Of course," I said. Because, yeah sure. Why not? But what did that even mean?

I must have said some part of that last bit aloud, because Thanatos answered me.

"Surely you've been here enough times to know that shadows in this realm are the souls of those who cast them?"

"They are?"

"Of course. Why else would yours be part dragon, part snow leopard, and part… that other thing?"

I turned my head slightly, trying to actually focus on my shadow, and then promptly looked away. It was kind of nauseating to see that many different creatures trying to take up the same space. Then, out of morbid curiosity, I glanced at Thanatos' shadow, and looked away even faster. The clam-Cthulhu hybrid was not a fun thing to see, even as a two dimensional shape, and it looked especially strange melded with something like a winged human.

"Ok," I sighed, deciding that I shouldn't even try looking at Trev's shadow, all things considered. "So does that mean you ate Albert's soul, as well?"

Thanatos shrugged his tiny blue bunny shoulders. A strange motion on a rabbit, but whatever. He wasn't really a rabbit, when it came down to it.

"I only tasted one…flavor, if you will. So I don't think he was in there. Not that that helps, mind you. If he's not in there, then you may not have any luck returning him to his body before it dies completely."

"I… what?"

"I would recommend getting that body back to earth as quickly as you can. If your friend is still able to reclaim the body, you have very little time for him to do it. It may already be too late."

WHICH IS WHY, a few seconds later, I was slapping Trev awake (or trying to) in the middle of MOME's dank Phoenix dungeons, ignoring how many times I kept repeating the same damned loop in favor of more pressing issues.

Unlike a dark-matter-suppressed Gwen, Albert was a full-grown man who didn't seem to be any lighter thanks to the dungeon's special properties. I was gonna need help carrying him.

"Gwendamnit," I cried, slapping Trev again, and really starting to worry.

"Now what?" Gwen asked, causing me to almost drop Trev in surprise.

"Damn it, Gwen, you shouldn't be down here, it can hurt you!"

She shrugged and then glared at me.

"I'm a goddess," she said, tossing her ridiculous red curls at me.

"This place almost killed you last time," I said, and something about my tone, or maybe the panic in my eyes, must have gotten her attention because she put a hand on my shoulder.

"We're almost clear of the dark matter suppressing rocks here, Vic. It takes more than this place to cut me off from my power. It hurts, but it won't do anything terrible unless I stay here for a while. I assume we're not planning on staying?" she said, nodding at my two, unconscious companions.

But I couldn't respond. All I could do was stare mutely at her in horror.

"Vic?"

"Past the dark matter suppressing rocks?"

"Yeah, almost, why?"

"Gwen, am I about to explode?"

"What? Why would you explode?"

"Because I was injected with Technetium just before—"

"Vic, darling, you were *not* injected with Technetium.

"I wasn't? But I felt the needle—"

"No."

"How can you be sure?"

"Because, if you *had* been injected you'd already be dead by now, along with everyone else in this city. The dark matter suppressers here aren't effective enough to keep you safe from Technetium, unlike that canyon you keep visiting."

Oddly, that didn't make me feel much better because it meant that I had put everyone I loved at risked just by returning to earth. Then I blinked and looked down at Albert's prone form on the stone floor and realized if I wasn't going to accidentally kill everyone I needed to refocus on the problem at hand.

"We need to get Albert back to wherever Dryer left his soul," I said, as if she should just know what that meant.

Gwen looked at Albert and then back at me.

"I don't think that's how this works, Vic," she said, and the gentleness in her voice made my blood run cold in my veins.

"Gwen, you have to do something. We can't just let him die. Dryer possessed him and then a demon ate her soul and..." my voice trailed off, but Gwen's eyes just looked sad.

"Fine," I said, not having patience for whatever she believed was going on here. "Just get the three of us out of this damned dark matter suppressing dungeon and *I'll* fix it."

"Vic, I don't think—"

"Just GET US OUT OF HERE!"

Gwen didn't reply, she just grabbed my arm, and Albert's (I was already holding Trev's) and shifted us.

~~~

The next moment we were in one of the horribly lit linoleum hallways of upper MOME. They were, as they had been the last few times I'd traversed them, abandoned. I looked at Gwen, and she looked at Albert and then at Trev.

"Want me to take your brother to his dragon mate?" she asked.

I nodded, not sure I could speak without screaming or crying. Trev was still unconscious, but he was breathing normally, and I didn't think there was much I could do for him aside from getting Gwen take him somewhere else. Rhelia could heal him if he needed it, and would protect him, or ask Gwen to, if necessary.

"Souls don't just come back to bodies, Vic."

"What if I take him to Life and—"

"Life can't fix anything without a soul in residence, and that's Albert's only problem right now. Otherwise he's uninjured."

She was gone as soon as the words left her mouth, Trev in tow.
~~~

I stared at Albert's inert form for a moment, hoping beyond hope that Gwen was just wrong. That being possessed meant that Albert's soul was just kicking it nearby somewhere, and would return to him soon. But the seconds ticked by, and his body just got paler and paler and...

Suddenly I was on my knees next to Albert's body, with my forehead pressed to his.

"How do I fix this, Albert? How do I help you? Where is your soul!?"

Of course he didn't answer me.

But something did.

A memory. My memory. I closed my eyes, trying to relax and let my brain get the message through. Three versions of me sitting around a room that didn't exist in anything but my imagination. Or else, didn't exist outside of my dark matter. Albert wasn't in his body anymore, but that didn't mean he was gone completely. He could just be stuck. I had been stuck once.

And before I could consider what a terrible idea this probably was, before I could remind myself that only luck and my connection to Trev had saved me the last time, before my brain could explain that what I was about to do should be impossible anyway, I was holding onto Albert's shoulders for dear life and reaching into time and space, not following my own dark matter, but reaching for Albert's instead.

~~~

"How interesting," said a voice that filled me with an enormous sense of relief. "By all accounts, this should not be possible."

I looked up into the friendly grey-blue gaze of Albert Bumblebee.

"Yeah, Gwen tried to tell me I couldn't save you. Still not sure this is going to work," I replied.

Albert simply stared at me for a moment.

"But your body is dying, so we should probably get a move on," I added.

"This space is generally devoid of time," Albert replied, still blinking slowly at my sudden arrival.

The room we were in looked an awful lot like Albert's office at school, with a few major differences. It had windows that looked out onto a decidedly English-looking countryside, and there were no iguanas draped over the backs of the red velvet wingback chairs here. I kinda missed them. To my amazement, as soon as I longed for the sight of one, a six-foot-long iguana appeared, already draped languidly across the back of a wingback.
~~~

Albert blinked at it for a moment, before turning to me again.

I figured it was best if I didn't ask, so I just replied to Albert's last statement about time.

"That's been my experience with my personal dimensional pocket too, but you came here without your body as an anchor this time, so I'm not sure that's true anymore. I mean, you were a lifeless corpse when I left you. Luckily, you've been that way for less than two minutes, but we are starting to push the boundaries of 'how long a body can survive while technically dead,' and I really don't want to get back from here and find out we're too late."

Albert smiled.

"But, my dear girl, you've brought the tether with you already. I can feel that I'm once more connected to myself."

"Seriously? It was that easy?" I looked around bewildered.

"I would not call it easy," Albert said, arching a white eyebrow in my direction. "I've never heard of anyone accomplishing such a task before. Besides, we've yet to make it out of here. I can feel that the tether to my body is restored, but I've no idea what to do with it. I'm not supposed to be in this place."

"So you've never been here before?" I asked.

"No. I've placed other things here, but I cannot venture here myself without becoming trapped. I rather thought this was simply what death was. Rebecca pushed me out of my body rather forcefully, when I wasn't expecting it. I was certain this was to be my afterlife."

"Ok. Weird. If our afterlife is getting trapped in our own pocket dimension, I really don't want to die."

Albert shrugged.

"There were plenty of good books," he said.

I looked around at his shelves and considered it.

"Only ones you'd read before, though, right?"

Albert looked at his shelves for a moment.

"Fair point. Let's get out of here, shall we?"

I nodded, reaching out a hand to Albert. If he didn't know how to get out of here, I was probably going to have to help. I suppose it made sense, as Albert didn't have any experience shifting into animal form by reaching for a body that was familiar to him.

Reminding myself that I had gotten stuck before because I'd been in a dimensional pocket with all of my own forms, I figured the easiest way out of here was probably going to be shifting to one of those. I closed my eyes, even though that was arguably unnecessary, and thought of being coated in thick fur, having a hefty tail to check my balance, and padding along on four padded feet that could run over snow and rocks.

I returned to the awful fluorescence that was the MOME hallway I'd just left, and blinked.

Then I jumped back and hissed when I was confronted with a six-foot-long iguana.

And no Albert.

"Umm…" I had apparently shifted back to human for the sole purpose of speaking. Because, holy shit, what had I done?

The iguana looked at me and blinked a few times, seemingly undisturbed and unsurprised by my presence, both as cat and human.

"Albert?" I asked, wondering if I was hallucinating, or somehow still stuck in a pocket dimension. Or maybe just a very odd hell realm.

The iguana opened its mouth, as though to speak, but it merely wheezed and hissed a bit before snapping its mouth shut again.

A moment later, Albert stood before me where the iguana had been.

"Well, that was educational," he said, before his legs gave out and he slid to the floor.

~~~
~~~

"Albert!" I shouted racing to his side. "Are you ok?"

Albert blinked a few more times, his gaze distant and unfocused, and his tongue darted out for a moment before sliding back into his mouth.

"I am alive, and I am not permanently an iguana," he answered.

"True statements," I replied, waiting for actual confirmation that he was ok.

"I believe that means I am ok. However, when this day is over, I have…a few questions for you, Vic. Everything that has happened in the past few minutes should not be possible."

"Ha! Welcome to my life," I said, giving Albert a hug, which he dazedly returned before getting back to his feet with a little help from my shoulders.

"Indeed," he said. "Let's go finish this, shall we?"

~~~

The next moment we were in one of the horribly lit linoleum hallways of upper MOME. They were, as they had been the last few times I'd traversed them, abandoned. I looked at Gwen, and she looked at Albert and then at Trev.

"Want me to take your brother to his dragon mate?" she asked.
~~~

I nodded, not sure I could speak without screaming or crying. Trev was still unconscious, but he was breathing normally, and I didn't think there was much I could do for him aside from getting Gwen take him somewhere else. Rhelia could heal him if he needed it, and would protect him, or ask Gwen to, if necessary.

"Souls don't just come back to bodies, Vic."

"What if I take him to Life and—"

"Life can't fix anything without a soul in residence, and that's Albert's only problem right now. Otherwise he's uninjured."

She was gone as soon as the words left her mouth, Trev in tow.

I stared at Albert's inert form for a moment, hoping beyond hope that Gwen was just wrong. That being possessed meant that Albert's soul was just kicking it nearby somewhere, and would return to him soon. But the seconds ticked by, and his body just got paler and paler and…

Suddenly I was on my knees next to Albert's body, with my forehead pressed to his.

"How do I fix this, Albert? How do I help you? Where is your soul!?"

Of course he didn't answer me.

But something did.

A memory. My memory. I closed my eyes, trying to relax and let my brain get the message through. Three versions of me sitting around a room that didn't exist in anything but my imagination. Or else, didn't exist outside of my dark matter. Albert wasn't in his body anymore, but that didn't mean he was gone completely. He could just be stuck. I had been stuck once.

And before I could consider what a terrible idea this probably was, before I could remind myself that only luck and my connection to Trev had saved me the last time, before my brain could explain that what I was about to do should be impossible anyway, I was holding onto Albert's shoulders for dear life and reaching into time and space, not following my own dark matter, but reaching for Albert's instead.

~~~

"How interesting," said a voice that filled me with an enormous sense of relief. "By all accounts, this should not be possible."

I looked up into the friendly grey-blue gaze of Albert Bumblebee.

"Yeah, Gwen tried to tell me I couldn't save you. Still not sure this is going to work," I replied.
~~~

Albert simply stared at me for a moment.

"But your body is dying, so we should probably get a move on," I added.

"This space is generally devoid of time," Albert replied, still blinking slowly at my sudden arrival.

The room we were in looked an awful lot like Albert's office at school, with a few major differences. It had windows that looked out onto a decidedly English-looking countryside, and there were no iguanas draped over the backs of the red velvet wingback chairs here. I kinda missed them. To my amazement, as soon as I longed for the sight of one, a six-foot-long iguana appeared, already draped languidly across the back of a wingback.

Albert blinked at it for a moment, before turning to me again.

I figured it was best if I didn't ask, so I just replied to Albert's last statement about time.

"That's been my experience with my personal dimensional pocket too, but you came here without your body as an anchor this time, so I'm not sure that's true anymore. I mean, you were a lifeless corpse when I left you. Luckily, you've been that way for less than two minutes, but we are starting to push the boundaries of 'how long a body can survive while technically dead,' and I really don't want to get back from here and find out we're too late."

Albert smiled.

"But, my dear girl, you've brought the tether with you already. I can feel that I'm once more connected to myself."

"Seriously? It was that easy?" I looked around bewildered.

"I would not call it easy," Albert said, arching a white eyebrow in my direction. "I've never heard of anyone accomplishing such a task before. Besides, we've yet to make it out of here. I can feel that the tether to my body is restored, but I've no idea what to do with it. I'm not supposed to be in this place."

"So you've never been here before?" I asked.

"No. I've placed other things here, but I cannot venture here myself without becoming trapped. I rather thought this was simply what death was. Rebecca pushed me out of my body rather forcefully, when I wasn't expecting it. I was certain this was to be my afterlife."

"Ok. Weird. If our afterlife is getting trapped in our own pocket dimension, I really don't want to die."

Albert shrugged.

"There were plenty of good books," he said.

I looked around at his shelves and considered it. "Only ones you'd read before, though, right?"

Albert looked at his shelves for a moment.

"Fair point. Let's get out of here, shall we?"

I nodded, reaching out a hand to Albert. If he didn't know how to get out of here, I was probably going to have to help. I suppose it made sense, as Albert didn't have any experience shifting into animal form by reaching for a body that was familiar to him.

Reminding myself that I had gotten stuck before because I'd been in a dimensional pocket with all of my own forms, I figured the easiest way out of here was probably going to be shifting to one of those. I closed my eyes, even though that was arguably unnecessary, and thought of being coated in thick fur, having a hefty tail to check my balance, and padding along on four padded feet that could run over snow and rocks.

I returned to the the awful fluorescence that was the MOME hallway I'd just left, and blinked.

Then I jumped back and hissed when I was confronted with a six-foot-long iguana.

And no Albert.

"Umm…" I had apparently shifted back to human for the sole purpose of speaking. Because, holy shit, what had I done?

The iguana looked at me and blinked a few times, seemingly undisturbed and unsurprised by my presence, both as cat and human.

"Albert?" I asked, wondering if I was hallucinating, or somehow still stuck in a pocket dimension. Or maybe just a very odd hell realm.

The iguana opened its mouth, as though to speak, but it merely wheezed and hissed a bit before snapping its mouth shut again.

A moment later, Albert stood before me where the iguana had been.

"Well, that was educational," he said, before his legs gave out and he slid to the floor.

"Albert!" I shouted racing to his side. "Are you ok?"

Albert blinked a few more times, his gaze distant and unfocused, and his tongue darted out for a moment before sliding back into his mouth.

"I am alive, and I am not permanently an iguana," he answered.

"True statements," I replied, waiting for actual confirmation that he was ok.

"I believe that means I am ok. However, when this day is over, I have…a few questions for you, Vic. Everything that has happened in the past few minutes should not be possible."

"Ha! Welcome to my life," I said, giving Albert a hug, which he dazedly returned before getting back to his feet with a little help from my shoulders.

"Indeed," he said. "Let's go finish this, shall we?"

S SOON AS Albert was steady on his feet I shifted to dragon form, clutched Albert in one set of talons, and then shifted my dragon ass out to the front of the building, because running through those damned fluorescent hallways again could fucking die in a fire.

If I ever got ahold of the jackass who was supposed to be in charge of this story, I was going to slap them. Honestly, if I were a person reading my life right now, I would be losing my shit. How many times can one person run out the same set of doors into mortal peril, only to have to go right back to the same fucking hell dimension to avoid destroying the world, in one day? It was too much.

And whoever was writing this damned story must have thought so too, because when I broke through the doors this time, no one was trying to tear the universe into tiny pieces with an ill-advised magical bomb.

Nope.

They were just trying to kill all of my friends and family with regular old gunfire and spell-slinging.

It looked like things hadn't gone all that well after I'd left with Dryer/Albert and Trevor. MOME was still clearly trying to kill everybody I cared about, just not with any world-ending weapons. I took a moment to wonder who was leading this whole thing, with Dryer deposed, but I honestly wasn't sure that it mattered. In all likelihood, she had more than one lackey, or even a few other MOME higher-ups, who were probably all too happy to see all non-magical humans subjugated, magical entities becoming top dogs, and MOME themselves running the whole thing. Honestly, based on what I'd heard Albert and Sol say about the biases of the magic-wielding world in general, it probably hadn't even been that hard for Dryer to get people to see her "side" of things. In fact, now I was wondering if she'd actually faced more than token opposition.

So it probably shouldn't have been a surprise to find that the asshats I'd left behind when I'd tackled their leader into another dimension were still hard at it, trying to kill the rest of us. After all, a bunch of us had shown up to make it clear that we weren't in favor of the whole "subjugate all humans" piece. And, now, with all of the reinforcements that the Unterberg delegation seemed to have brought along, we had almost half as many fighters as MOME did, even without our suspiciously absent dragon reinforcements.

We'd clearly thrown a wrench in whatever attack plan MOME had for today. An invasion of some kind, if Rebecca Dryer's raving ghost was to be believed. So, yeah, they were probably more than a little pissed off at us.

And that was fine, really. I mean, what the hell? This was something we were all more or less equipped for, unlike ripping holes in the universe. I put Albert on the ground. He nodded and ran off to do whatever badass mages do in a fight, and I launched myself skyward. As I rose into the cerulean Phoenix sky, I took stock of the battle below.

The reinforcements from Unterberg were spread out, not far from where they'd been when I'd grabbed Trev and Albert/Dryer from certain doom, and many of them were flinging spells at MOME's leather-clad mages. They were doing a fair bit of damage, though their own shields were also taking plenty of hits.

In addition, the Unterbergers seemed to have a number of shifters, ogres, trolls, and other large hand-to-hand combatants, whose forms and names I was unfamiliar with, who were giving the MOME mages one hell of a time. The MOME mages were doing what they could to defend against a simultaneously magical and physical assault, but it seemed like they hadn't brought as many shifters to this battle, and they'd lost the advantage as a consequence.

As I rose higher, I caught sight of a huddle in my peripheral vision that included Seamus' Moms and my parents, along with a recently arrived Albert, all of whom seemed to be involved in a hurried discussion. I had to assume that it was a strategy meeting, but soon I lost sight of them in the fray and decided that I was needed elsewhere, anyway.

Rhelia, in her glorious dragon form, was tearing into a troop of mages with her talons and teeth, looking as furious as I'd ever seen her. And, as I dove down to join the fray, I saw Sol streak past in her panther form, knocking the guns from the hands of the few remaining mind control victims who were still running on instructions to kill us, deftly dodging bullets as she went. Rhelia must have spread the word about not killing the front line grunts.

Seamus, much to my surprise, was tearing around in wolf form, dragging something long and wet from his mouth and sneaking up behind troops to hit them with it. I had no idea what that was about, and I didn't have time to figure it out before I reached the fight and started tearing into a line of mages at Rhelia's side.

I gave Rhelia plenty of space, assuming that her attack radius would need to include her tail, and trying to account for how much larger she was than me. Of course, I hadn't really accounted for how she would react to me coming back without Trev. Thankfully, she didn't actually tear into me, the way her shrieking dive in my direction made me fear. Instead, she stopped short and turned on the mages to my side.

Where issss he? He issss not resssssponding to my call.

I batted a few MOME mages aside with my tail as I replied, *He's safe, but I can't get ahold of him either.*

To be honest, I hadn't even thought of communicating with him mentally until Rhelia had started diving at me, and it had occurred to me that she might want an answer about where Trev was. But he hadn't replied to my very urgent suggestions that now would be a great time to wake up, you know, *before* his girlfriend/soulmate/ partner eviscerated me. So, I wasn't lying when I told Rhelia that he wasn't replying to me either.

Rhelia turned aside briefly to literally bite a MOME mage in half, and I was grateful that I was in my dragon form, because dragon-me wasn't nearly as squeamish as human-me, and I was pretty sure human-me would have tossed her cookies at that.

Wassss he harmed? Her mental voice was surprisingly calm now, despite how anxious she'd seemed just a moment ago.

Not after we got to hell, I replied, casually swatting a few more MOME mages away with my foreleg before they could launch their spells at me. Damn, it was handy to be able to see magic. It was even more handy to know that the majority of it was just going to bounce off of my scales. *I have no idea what Dryer did to him before I grabbed him, though. I didn't get there until just before she tried to inject him.*

I thought sssshe had merely put a ssssleep sssspell on him, but that sssshould have worn off with her demisssse.

She turned and roared in the faces of a group of about six mages who were trying to sneak up on her, and I swear more than half of them soiled themselves as they retreated. I tried not to take too many deep breaths, as I didn't really want to confirm that one.

Where is he? Rhelia asked again, after the mages had retreated.

I gave him to Gwen. I didn't know what else to do with him. I couldn't leave him unconscious and alone in the hell realms, I replied, trying to keep the annoyance out of my voice.

It hadn't really occurred to me to leave him behind. I didn't consider Thanatos, who could apparently eat people's souls even in his blue bunny form, to be a safe person to leave my unconscious twin with, and there hadn't been time to do anything else.

My thoughts must have leaked to Rhelia anyway.

I am sure Gwen will keep him safe.

I couldn't help but notice that Rhelia's accent was slipping again, and I wondered if it slipped when she was annoyed, or just when shit got serious enough that she didn't want to waste time on the extra sibilance.

We were both momentarily distracted by a barrage of spells that included a few of the nastier, dragon-scale-breaching variety, so we dodged in silence for a moment, before resuming our own attacks and our conversation.

A small part of me just wanted to end all of this nonsense with dragon fire, then bring Thanatos in to do the cleanup and call it good, but something told me that if it were as easy as I thought it was, someone else already would have suggested it.

I'm not sure where Gwen took him, but it's got to be safer than here, right? I said, after charging, bull-style, straight into about a dozen mages and sending them flying. I saw a few of their shields wink out on impact, and I wondered if that meant they would stay down. Human-me was worried I'd killed them. Dragon-me, honestly, wasn't. I brushed aside the worry that there seemed to be a distinction between the two mes as something that I could figure out later.

I can try calling Gwen and ask her to bring him to you, I added, since I could tell Rhelia was still a bit tense, and I didn't want her to think that I didn't understand just how worried she was about Trev.

Rhelia snorted a few tendrils of smoke.

I trust her to care for him. I am merely upset that he is missing this fight. I believe he will be upset not to have participated.

I laughed, accidentally incinerating the mage who'd been charging at me with an actual, honest-to-Gwen, flaming sword.

Luckily, it was only a short burst of flame, and somehow managed not to light anything else on fire. Weirdly, the sword continued to burn, even after the charred top half of the mage disintegrated and the legs toppled awkwardly after it.

Good shot; that sword would have pierced even the thickest dragon hide. Rhelia's praise was casual, albeit sincere, as if I'd done that on purpose. As if I'd somehow known that the sword was deadly to dragons, and not like I'd accidentally just laughed and killed a man. The human part of me felt a bit queasy, but the human part of me was decidedly not in charge right now, so maybe I *had* known. Maybe that hadn't been as much of an accident as I'd thought.

And then I didn't care whether it was an accident or not, because something had just shanked me in the shin. Or rather, I discovered as I looked down, someone had just bitten one of my forelegs. The "someone" was a vampire, that was clear enough, and apparently vampire teeth were another thing (besides flaming swords) that could pierce through dragon hide. Not that it felt like it was doing much damage, since vampires are quite a bit smaller than dragons, even a baby dragon like me.

I reared up on my back legs and shook my foreleg fiercely. The vamp did not let go.

I turned and battered him against the side of one of the concrete parking barriers nearby.

He still didn't let go.

I slammed my foreleg into the ground.

He was still there.

The whole thing was starting to piss me off. It barely hurt, but having a vampire stuck to my leg was not going to help this fight, and besides, I'd felled a vamp in my human form before with a solid knee to the nuts. What the hell was letting this vampire cling to me like the world's angriest Corgi in beast mode?

I didn't know how he was doing it, but I'd just decided I was going to show him who was running this show, when I felt a few more sharp pains along my back legs and sides.

The fuck?

I craned my long neck around to stare down at a good dozen vampires sticking to me, even as I began dancing around trying to shake them off. Those damned diamond skulls must give them the jaw strength of snapping turtles. They. Weren't. Coming. OFF!

I had just taken in a breath to douse the one on my arm in dragon fire, when I remembered the burns on my sides and arms from the damned tank I'd lit on fire. They were still sore, despite my Az-boost and sped up healing. So I shot a bunch of smoke out of my nostrils, instead of the burst of fire I'd been considering releasing.

Fine. If these assholes wanted to leech onto me, they could just try to stick around while I—

My legs collapsed beneath me like jello.

What. The. Fuck?

My eyelids started to droop, my head dipping slowly towards my chest, leaving my neck closer to the ground, though none of the vamps let go of their holds to take advantage of it.

Help, I sent out to Rhelia, or whoever was close by that could hear mental communication. For once, I was *trying* to broadcast.

Rhelia must have been busy.

No one replied.

My eyelids drooped a little bit more. My head sank lower to the ground.

Then my vision began to tunnel, and all the sounds of battle dropped away.

Then silver feathers, and the faint sounds of someone screaming.

Huh. Sounded painful.

I'M NOT SURE how I'd managed to forget how efficient Azrael was when it came to killing vampires. I mean, they had taken out Edik in about ten seconds. And ok, yeah, that hadn't stuck, but they'd also managed to incapacitate a room full of vamps in about 90 seconds.

Whatever. A lot had happened since Az had said they loathed vampires, and I'd kinda forgotten it in the insanity of everything that had happened afterwards, but I wasn't likely to ever forget it again.

My eyes popped open after the first few vampires released me, and I got to watch, in stunned awe, as Azrael took out the remaining vampires. Az was stunning to look at normally, no matter which of their forms they took (as long as it wasn't red naked squirrel form), but now, as they swooped from vamp to vamp, draining the vamps' energy so that each one collapsed to the ground looking like nothing more than an attractive corpse, they were positively glowing. No, literally. Az was exuding light like an exuberantly decorated Christmas tree. Or maybe a lightning bug hopped up on coke, since they were zigging and zagging faster than my eye could track, and vibrating with…something. Souls? Life force?

That was the only thing I could come up with, because I knew Az fed off of people's souls, and the vamps that were now falling like moths that had gotten too close to a flame seemed…drained, empty, colorless.

Of course, that was probably how any animated corpse that had lost its animation looked, but still.

Az was exuding power like a flying torch.

Something about the vamps releasing me had returned enough energy to me to let me open my eyes and turn my head, but it wasn't until all the vamps had dropped, and Az swooped past me to plant a steaming kiss on my scaled snout, that I felt strong enough to stand up.

That kiss felt like a living flame. I wasn't just restored. I was on fire, and I realized that a dozen vamps worth of energy must have been quite the power hit, because Az had glow to spare and they were more than happy to share it with me.

I felt the energy spread through my body like a wildfire, and I flapped my wings in exultation, looking around the field of battle for a new target.

But then an orange streak in the sky caught my eye, and I looked up just in time to see Trev, in Phoenix form, dive-bomb another group of MOME mages who had been about to take aim at Rhelia.

Well, damn. I had no idea what had finally woken Trev up, but he seemed to be fine. I felt something untwist inside me, and realized that I'd been more worried about Trev than I'd let myself admit, even once he was safely under Gwen's protection.

Az had already flown away and returned to the fight before I could even utter a thank you.

Time to get back into the fight.

I didn't see any more conscious vampires anywhere, so dragon-me's intense desire for vengeance was just going to have to wait for a bit. Meanwhile, Az's brightly glowing form was flitting all over the place wreaking havoc wherever they went.

Rhelia was tearing into the mages with abandon, with Trev's assistance, and I was about to join her.

Meanwhile, every now and again I saw what looked like wisps of smoke appear around a person carrying a gun, and then that person seemed to disappear. Which explained why I hadn't seen Renata lately, and why there were very few mind control victims left.

We were still outnumbered almost two to one, despite having wiped out a good portion of MOME's mage forces in the past few minutes, and even with two dragons on our side, that still seemed like a lot.

I could only assume that the main reason they hadn't attacked en masse again was because we'd killed the majority of the leadership. Which raised the question of why they were attacking at all.

And also made me wonder why we still *only* had two dragons.

General Aira has refused to issue reinforcements. Rhelia's mental voice sounded pissed, and I couldn't honestly blame her. *She is keeping herself and our army hidden in a pocket dimension until ready to be deployed.*

Did she give a reason for that? I asked.

She claimed to be holding our forces in strategic reserve. Rhelia's mental communication managed to convey all her disdain for that plan, without any additional words.

Do you think she's betrayed us, somehow? I asked, not sure how she could have, or if she would have, but feeling like that was just the way today was going.

Rhelia sent the mental equivalent of a shrug.

Right. Ok. Super reassuring.

But then I didn't have time to think about all the shitty potential consequences of betrayal by the commander of our own reinforcements, because I was busy batting away another handful of mages who had decided to consolidate their power and send something truly nasty my way. Except, I sent those mages flying before the spell finished forming, causing their half-formed spell to ricochet off the spell of a second set ofu nearby mages and scatter everyone in a three-meter radius. The first spell had still been just an amorphous blob, and it latched onto one of the mages and sent him screaming, thrashing, and running away from the group. The other spell showed a striking re-semblance to Thanatos in his Cthulhu/clam form, and it started devouring the nearby mages indi-scriminately. It looked like I had knocked both groups out of their containment circles, which was great for distracting the mages and perhaps getting them eaten by demons, but I kinda doubted that whatever demons had been summoned were going to just call it a day after they'd devoured the mages who'd summoned them. Especially when the thing that looked like Thanatos expanded to its full size, which, yeah…either there was more than one clam/Cthulhu-dark-matter-consuming-demon in the world, or that *was* Thanatos.

Although, since he hadn't exploded and taken us all down with him, I was willing to consider that it was maybe just Thanatos' cousin or something.

Then the thing turned its crazy, protruding eyes at me, and waved a tentacle in my general direction.

Huh, maybe it was Thanatos after all. Or maybe…

Maybe that was just a distraction to keep me from launching myself at yet another MOME recruit, who was busy stabbing the amorphous blob with a syringe on the far side of the parking lot. Far out of my reach.

Pushing the plunger in before I could so much as take one step forward.

UCH TO MY surprise, I wasn't dead. A quick look around the area proved that most everyone I loved also was not dead. I still didn't understand why the few MOME lackeys I'd run into who had tried to inject people I love with Technetium seemed to think there was even the slightest chance that a hazmat suit might protect them.

Because what I'd just witnessed was horrifying, and had definitely killed the guy who injected the blob with Technetium—who had *not* been wearing a hazmat suit, not that I thought it would have helped—but at least it wasn't the insane, world-ending event that I had expected.

The blob had exploded in spectacular fashion. It was more a light show than an explosion really, like someone had put a billion microscopic Christmas lights into a piñata and then shot it with a Death Star. It absolutely incinerated the MOME guy with the syringe, as well as everyone else in a radius of about ten meters of the demon who'd been injected. Which, as far as I could tell, had consisted solely of more MOME agents.

It was difficult to tell, if only because I was still blinking away the blinding points of light. And also because the dozen MOME mages weren't the only casualties of the event.

Time and space seemed to have taken a hit as well.

Because, holy shit, as if my ears had suddenly come back online after a brief delay, there was a brain-shearing sound, like the rending of a million sheets of tinfoil all at once.

And then I could see an orange sky with a purple sun, still framed by our blue sky with its white-yellow sun; a sight that was enough to make me feel nauseous on its own, but it didn't end there. Nope. It did not.

Because out of the desert under the orange sky with the purple sun poured hundreds, possibly a thousand or more, demons.

And, ok, maybe now I understood what Dryer had meant, when she was raving about being knee deep in bodies thanks to an invasion…

It was difficult to tell how many there were, because they were all changing shape as soon as they tumbled through the tear in the seam and onto Earth. Beings that started out as furless squirrels, furry bunnies, tiny goats, poofy owls, fuzzy otters, strange ducks, and a whole host of other mostly harmless looking animals poured into earth as creatures straight out of nightmares, bringing the pungent scent of sulphur with them.

A small handful, perhaps the other succubi, appeared angelic as they flew through the bright Phoenix sky, giant feathered wings on the backs of gorgeous humanoids, but the majority took on forms that had too many limbs, tentacles, or proboscises to count, all of which were attached to giant, fang-filled maws, or horrible suctioning mouths, or, ew, honestly, it was getting too gross for me to keep track of.

"Well, fuck," I was startled to hear myself say aloud.

I was back in human form, though I'd made no conscious decision to switch. I would have liked to take the time to wonder about that: had the rip in the seam knocked me into my human form? How did that even work? But the creatures were stumbling through the tear in the seam in droves, and immediately setting upon, well, everyone.

They were attacking MOME's forces, they were attacking our Unterberger allies, and in a moment I would love to scour from my retinae, but probably never will, I even saw Ms. Rebuke tear off her shirt and launch herself into the arms of a succubus, just before it took off into the sky and left the site of the battle entirely.

The demons were attacking our ranks, but they were also spilling away from our ridiculous battle and out into the streets that surrounded us, taking eager hold of the human population that I hadn't even noticed had been cowering behind whatever cover they could find in the area.

I'm not sure why the non-magical people nearby had felt that was a good idea—perhaps because we'd been very clearly focused on our own little battle and hadn't been making a point of ransacking the city or anything. People like a spectacle, and we sure as shit counted as one. Maybe they thought we were making a movie.

They were learning the price of that choice now, though, as the demons spilled forth and made no attempts to organize their attacks. In fact, they seemed to be plowing into the streets with reckless abandon, grabbing humans and throwing them into waiting fanged maws, or just throwing them into the sides of buildings, where they landed with sickening cracks.

'This is bad," I said to no one.

"No jodas," replied Sol in her standard monotone.

My relief at seeing her alive, in one piece, and well enough to make dark jokes was short lived. The demons just kept coming. The rip in the seam was as wide as the parking lot that it filled, and there were dozens more of them pouring through every second. We had to do something.

If only I had the faintest clue what.

"What do we do?" Seamus asked, appearing beside us and echoing my thoughts.

And ok, I couldn't help myself, I threw my arms around them both, unaware how much I'd missed them until they were both back in my sight again.

"We fight," Sol said, after a brief embrace, even though her face showed what a bleak prospect she thought that was.

I nodded, and Seamus' face paled, but his chin dipped with mine. What choice did we have? The demons were going to tear this place apart, and I didn't know how on Earth we were going to stop them, but I was starting to think some dragon fire might be in order. Just because Thanatos could eat it, that didn't mean it wouldn't kill most of the demons who had just poured through that tear.

So we stood, shoulder to shoulder, facing the horde of demons who had, for whatever reason, maybe because they'd been invited by MOME—*that* would be entirely like Dryer—or maybe just because they could, decided to take out Phoenix, and together, as though we shared an internal count, we pulled on our animal forms.

And came out on the other side as something entirely new.

¿QUE DEMONIOS?

Vic, Sol, WHAT THE HELLS IS GOING ON?

Um…I have no clue, but we don't really have time to—

And then we were charging into the fray as one because… well, we were one.

There was a horde of demons charging straight for us, so we didn't have time to sort out why the fuck we'd just shifted and come out as a giant dragon body—as big as any of the adult dragons we'd seen in the dragon realms—with three fucking heads, only one of which was a dragon's. The other two were, perhaps predictably—if you could ever *predict* turning into a giant, three-headed monster right out of someone's nightmare mythology without meaning to—a wolf and a panther. But I didn't even have time to process all of that before a few dozen demons reached us at the same time and started throwing various appendages and powers at us at once.

We responded to that as you might expect a giant three-headed monster to respond.

We burned the shit out of them.

Turns out crazy-assed pseudo-chimera-Vic-Sol-Seamus could breathe dragon fire out of *all three* mouths.

Fuck yeah!

I wasn't sure which one of us thought that. Maybe all three of us had. Because in addition to body slamming the front line of demons that had charged us, we'd just used all three of our heads to light up the majority of the ones that were still standing (as well as quite a few of the ones who'd gone down).

We let out a roar that actually shook the pavement where we were standing, and shattered a few office building windows in the block around us.

That was about when the demons decided to take us more seriously.

At least, I assume that's why a surge of demons all attempted to attack us at the same time.

I couldn't count how many tried to overwhelm us, but my field of vision was nothing but demon.

Tentacles, claws, fangs, tongues, arms, legs, and a hundred other appendages I had no name for.

We were in an ocean of demons, and it felt like we were about to drown. The sheer press of that many other bodies on top of us, many of which seemed to be trying to drain our energy, was nearly overwhelming. We snapped our jaws and roared our defiance, but the press just kept coming. Pushing us down, down, down, against the hot concrete, under the bright September sun. A wave of dizziness swept us and our legs started to buckle.

But we weren't having that. Oh no. We were not.

Rise. One voice inside us, and our legs tightened against the strain.

These demons were going to learn what it meant to invade Earth.

Rise. Two voices in unison within us. Legs straightening against the horde, and three heads rising above the press.

Yes, they were going to learn, and MOME was going to learn what it meant to try to subjugate humans. And damn it all, this was going to stop.

Rise! Three voices together, and three heads raised to the sky, roaring in defiance and turning to spread flaming death wherever it was needed.

Our thoughts had largely melded, and I really couldn't tell who was thinking what, but none of us were objecting to any of the decisions being made. And our legs pushed against the onslaught of demons and our teeth started rending any flesh nearby that wasn't already in flames. And we drove ourselves forward, cutting a swath of destruction with each step, until the demons were scrambling to get out of our way.

Then our legs carried us towards the largest demon of the lot, which—you guessed it—was the one that looked like Cthulhu and a clam's gory love child.

THANATOS!!! We roared mentally, along with another physical roar that broke glass somewhere in the neighborhood.

And, apparently, Thanatos understood we were coming for him, because he turned his two creepy proboscis-like eyes towards us, and then dropped the tank he had been about to swallow (and yeah, he was as big as some of the buildings around us now, but that was ok, because we were even bigger) and I guess he decided that we would be an even tastier snack, because the next thing we knew, a giant tentacle was trying to wrap itself around our enormous midsection.

So we sprayed Thanatos with three heads worth of dragon fire.

Which *he* seemed to think was like bathing in chocolate or some shit, because he basically just rolled around and basked in it—absorbing it through his skin somehow—his hold around our midsection only tightening.

Which was when we decided to see how his tentacles held up against dragon fangs, wolf fangs, and panther fangs.

The answer was: not well.

He may have been used to fighting creatures with sharp fangs at a much smaller size, because, sure, when you grew to the size of a city block, a regular-sized panther wasn't going to do much but feel like a mosquito bite. But when the panther jaws in question were as large as a semi truck, that shit was going to sever your tentacles, no matter how much dragon fire they could absorb.

Which was when Thanatos' Cthulhu/clam-ass started to look nervous. He was down three tentacles now, and while he seemed to have plenty more where those came from, he did not have an infinite supply.

Meanwhile, we were not running out of teeth anytime soon.

He released our midsection and tried a new strategy, namely wrapping each of our three necks in tentacles. Admittedly, that would probably have been a good move, but he wasn't fast enough. Each of our necks and jaws snapped at the tentacles wending their way towards us, severing them each time before they ever managed to grab hold of us. We had taken off another five tentacles before Thanatos started backing away, using his largest remaining tentacles to help move things along, while its creepy clam tongue pushed it back towards the tear in the seam.

And that, of course, was when General Aira finally decided that we were worth reinforcing after all. I could hear the roar of a hundred dragons behind me, followed quickly by the terrified sounds of a few hundred demons freaking the fuck out.

Suddenly, Thanatos wasn't the only one beating a hasty retreat.

The tear in the seam, orange sky framed by blue, loomed larger than ever, now that we'd gotten quite a bit closer to it, and I/we could finally see that it was outlined by a faint red glow that flared and faded in certain areas. The red glow actually looked like a shredded curtain, if curtains were made out of shimmering red light, instead of fabric. Bits and pieces of it hung from above and below in tatters.

Then we were distracted from the rip in space-time by watching Thanatos get closer and closer to the tear between the two worlds, along with all the demons who'd been close enough to him to notice his retreat. It didn't seem like any official retreat had been called, though. A huge host of demons were still plowing their way through the torn seam into our realm, even as half of those that had arrived in the earlier waves were viciously attempting to push their way back through the crowd, most showing little regard for the well-being of their fellow demons who hadn't made it through the tear yet. I saw more than a few limbs, tentacles, and mandibles go flying in various directions as the two throngs collided.

I was relieved that some of the demons were retreating, but it was becoming increasingly clear that if we couldn't close this seam, we had no way to ensure that the whole host wouldn't be back as soon as they'd had a chance to regroup.

With surprising unanimity, we launched ourselves skyward sharply and then dove with single-minded fury for the clam/Cthulhu creature getting ready to slither back into his home realm.

Thanatos apparently hadn't been expecting that, or else he'd been too focused on pushing his way back through his fellow demons to notice our approach. We snapped down around him with a force that shattered a few car and office windows nearby, and sent many smaller demons tumbling away from us. I don't think we stepped on any, but I didn't really check.

Where ya headed, Bunny? we asked, hoping he understood this form of communication. I wasn't entirely sure how he was going to reply, since clams didn't exactly have vocal chords, but…

Please! Don't attack! I wish to negotiate!

Looked like we didn't have to worry about tentacle sign language after all.

Funny, it looks like you want to run away, not negotiate.

Yes, well, I had hoped to run away, but if you're going to pin me here and threaten to rip off all of my remaining limbs, I'd rather negotiate.

And, yeah, I could kinda see where he was coming from with that.

Do you surrender? we asked.

Yes! Most emphatically.

Then call an official retreat. Order the rest of the demons back into the hell realm you came from.

Well…I'm not technically in charge of them, you see, I'm more like—

All three of our heads snapped at Thanatos' proboscis eyes, roaring.

I suggest you exercise your leadership skills, we growled.

Erm…yes. Quite.

Thanatos' tentacles waved manically for a bit, then he made a series of strange trumpeting noises, and… well, not much changed. At least, not immediately. Some of the nearest demons piling through the seam stopped and tried to turn around, but the ones behind them just plowed into them and pushed them through. However, the roar of dragons increased behind us, and soon it wasn't just Thanatos' cries that were egging his fellows on. He made the same weird bugling call again, and that, accompanied by the fiery death being rained down behind us, seemed to seal the deal. The demons who were trying to push their way through to our realm finally noticed that our realm was no longer the free buffet they'd likely been promised, and those who hadn't already been leaving attempted to disengage with whoever they were fighting and make their retreat. An attempt that was aided by the fact that MOME's forces were quickly becoming overwhelmed by our newly arrived dragon army.

Is that acceptable? Thanatos asked, still doing his best to shrink back into his shell.

We didn't release him, but I nodded the dragon head, while the wolf and panther remained within close range of a few of his tentacles.

Now promise that you won't be returning here.

You cannot cut my people off from Earth! We would starve if we could never venture here.

I'm not saying your people can never come here, if they stick to whatever rules bound them before today. I'm saying, never come here as an army. Never another invasion. I don't care how wide a hole some asshat tears in your seam. You stay back and enjoy the view without sending in an army.

And what if some "asshat," as you call them, decides to invade our realm?

If that happens, and it's an unprovoked attack, you are welcome to defend yourself. You can even call on me for backup.

That response got a few warning rumbles from Sol and Seamus, so I decided to clarify.

And when I say "me," I mean Vic. I can't promise that Sol or Seamus will answer your call.

I couldn't fault them for not wanting to jump into a cordial relationship with Thanatos. I was wary of it too, but I had a feeling that Thanatos—as cunning as I was sure he was capable of being—hadn't been the mastermind behind this plan. He seemed to have gone out of his way to attack MOME wherever possible, plus he'd eaten Dryer's soul at the first chance he'd gotten. I didn't know much about how demon summoning worked, but I had a sneaking suspicion that he'd done what he could to help me today, and while I didn't particularly like the guy, I didn't think making an enemy of one of the most powerful demons in the hell realms was a good plan either.

My offer of help made Thanatos cease his constant twitching, for a moment. Then, to my eternal shock, the clam/Cthulhu hybrid beneath us blinked out of existence and was replaced with an imposing winged figure, very much like Az's, but only male (as far as I could see), and with golden skin and charcoal colored wings. Thick black hair fell in curls around his shoulders, and his eyes shone gold in the sunlight.

"You continue to surprise me, Vic," the nine-foot-tall winged man declared, flapping his wings until he was hovering more or less at dragon snout level.

I snorted a bit of smoke out of my nostrils, not wanting to incinerate anyone at the moment, and gave the dragon equivalent of a shrug.

Join the club, I projected to this winged Thanatos, hoping he could still understand me. *I hardly know what I'm going to do or say, half the time.*

"Ha! That may be true, but it is not your choice of words that surprises me. You have had multiple opportunities to destroy that which you did not understand today, and yet, every time, you have chosen… to treat me and my people with respect."

Um… did you miss the part where we wiped out a few dozen demons? I asked, cursing my own honesty. I mean, if Thanatos had somehow missed that part, I really shouldn't be the one to point it out to him.

"You did what anyone would do when their home is attacked. But you also offered us more mercy than we deserved, given the circumstances, and you didn't attempt to kill a small blue rabbit when you had the chance, even once you realized what I was."

I didn't really have a response for that. It was true, though I hadn't done it out of some higher sense of honor, I just… why would I kill someone who wasn't trying to kill me?

You should have seen how long it took her to get fatally pissed off at Edik.

And, ok, it seemed like Seamus could project our thoughts too in this form. I guess that only made sense.

Thanatos merely chuckled.

"Do you require any assistance in restraining the remaining forces from MOME?" he asked, casually, like he was offering to help clear the dishes after a potluck.

Nah, I think we've got this, I replied, before an idea struck me. *Unless… unless you know who has been leading the MOME forces since we got rid of Dryer? That would save us a whole lot of time.*

Thanatos smirked, nodded, and then shot up into the sky and out of sight.

I HAD JUST enough time to wonder if I'd made a terrible mistake when Thanatos shifted his angle, pinned his wings back to his sides, and dove through the mildly hazy Phoenix sky with alarming speed. He flared his wings just in time to avoid colliding with a flaming set of concrete barriers that appeared to have been turned into some kind of command post, and then fluttered gracefully inside it.

A few moments later, he popped back up with a screaming, flailing, balding man, who I was quite startled to recognize as the short dude who had been aiming a wand at me when I first pushed out the door of MOME at the beginning of this fight.

Which should have been impossible.

Because I had burned that man to ash.

A fact that was quickly explained when Thanatos brought the screaming, flailing man into our hearing range.

"WE HAD A DEAL! THAT WITCH KILLED MY BROTHER! YOU CAN'T DO THIS TO ME! I'LL DESTROY YOU ALL! I'LL MAKE MORE TECHNETIUM AND TEAR THIS WORLD APART! I—"

I was fairly certain that the man would have kept going for as long as we let him, but Thanatos shifted his grip on him, one of his hands venturing to the man's neck, performing some technique that caused his eyes to close and his head to loll to one side like a doll.

"This is what's left of MOME's security council—at least, of those who were bold enough to join the battle. I believe you'd already met his brother. Where would you like him?"

Again, Thanatos' tone was polite and casual, as though asking if I'd prefer this pile of dishes rinsed in the sink or placed straight into the dishwasher. And I was at a loss as to how to reply, because… what was I supposed to do with a prisoner of war? I wasn't part of any governing body. I didn't think I had permission to admit people into the dragon realms' prisons, even if Siara was technically my grandmother now, or whatever. Apparently, Sol and Seamus didn't have any great ideas either, and the silence was just getting awkward when Gwen materialized in midair, arm in arm with Albert.

"Oh good," she said, smiling. "You figured out the chimera trick."

Before I could react to *that* interesting tidbit, Albert spoke.

"Vic, Sol, Seamus, excellent to see you all in such fine form. Thanatos, I am less pleased to find you here, but I am… pleasantly surprised to see you corralling the vermin."

Nice to see you alive, Al, I projected, eliciting a small smile from Albert before he turned his full attention to Thanatos and the man he was holding.

"I think it would be best if you both came with me," he said, gesturing back towards the MOME building behind us.

I was honestly a bit surprised that the place was still standing. It was weird to think that so much destruction had been wrought since the start of this battle, but that most of it had missed the nondescript concrete building behind us.

"Vic, Sol, Seamus, you may, ahh…relax, if you feel the need," Albert said.

"Nice work saving the world," Gwen added, before she turned away with Albert's arm still linked in the crook of hers.

Then Thanatos flew off with the prisoner, whose name I hadn't even caught, and Albert and Gwen (and how could Gwen even fly?) floated off towards the front of the MOME building where Siara (who, last I'd checked, had been stranded on a cliff ledge in hell) was also waiting for them in her human form, along with the green-skinned, large-tusked woman from Unterberg, who I hadn't seen since we'd first been taken before the council there (who, for all I knew, was now in charge of Unterberg council, since Torrence and Nethia had been... otherwise occupied for a while now).

As our eyes scanned the battlefield, we realized that the fighting had completely stopped. The dragons arriving en masse had cowed even the most dedicated of MOME's forces, and now the field (or giant parking lot, as the case happened to be) was clearing to show the bodies of the fallen and the injured. Some people/demons were being carried off in various forms of restraint, and others were slinking back through the tear in the seam to the hell realm. A few bits of dragon fire smoldered away still, but there was another demon clam, much smaller than Thanatos, but similar in shape, sliding around eating the various flaming bits that littered the parking lot. As it was one of the only demons not retreating, and it seemed single-mindedly interested in dragon fire, I wasn't planning to argue. It was a harrowing scene, despite the relief I felt at seeing that the fighting was over. So much damage had been done, from the cars and buildings destroyed, to the people lying still all around us, some of whom must have been purely human, though you couldn't tell now who had been were, mage, or non, from the still forms that littered the ground.

And then, as suddenly as we'd become one, we stood next to each other in our human forms, three separate people, huddled against each other for comfort, reaching for one another with our arms even as our bodies regained their autonomy.

"Let's never do this again," Seamus muttered quietly.

"What, become a giant fire-breathing monster?" Sol asked, smiling.

"Nah," Seamus countered. "That part was badass. I was more talking about the whole war thing."

I laughed, and then choked on a sob.

"Yeah," I agreed, my voice cracking. "Let's skip that part next time."

THE NEXT FEW days, hell, the next few weeks, were a mess. A serious, life-altering mess for a lot of people.

To start with, I didn't know where Rhelia and Trevor had gone off to. I also hadn't seen Torrence lately, and a quick scan of the area around us didn't help. Az hadn't shown up since ridding me of a dozen vampires, and I couldn't see Seamus' parents, or mine, either.

Sol's Abuelita showed up to envelope her in a spine-crushing hug, and I decided that was my cue to sidle away, though Seamus gave me a wave that suggested he would stay and look for people.

I didn't particularly want to follow Albert and Gwen over to where a group of people who'd *actually finished high school*, not to mention actually understood most of the workings of the magical world, were about to make a bunch of decisions that would affect a huge number of people for a very long time. After all, I'd just fought, and bled, and risked Gwendamned everything, to save the world, and part of me thought I deserved a damned rest, and that those folks didn't actually need me. They could sort it out, and I could finally go take a nap. That part of me might even have been right, but a more vocal part of me insisted that I should at least make sure they got all the information they needed from me before I let myself relax. I had seen a bunch of shit that no one else had, and it might be relevant to figuring out how we should move forward from here.

As I gave Sol and Seamus one more hug, before turning towards the warded piece of concrete where our present leadership stood, I promised myself it would just be a few more minutes. That I would go debrief with the remaining leaders of the magical community, and then I would go home and take a three-day nap.

If only.

The first thing I did when I reached that group of magical leadership was throw my arms around Siara. Judging by how stiff she went in my embrace, she hadn't been expecting the move, but before I could back away and apologize for invading her space, she relaxed and returned the hug.

"How did you get here?" I asked, when I finally stepped away from her.

She laughed. "I'm afraid it's not a terribly exciting story. I waited until I felt my body had passed the Technetium from my system, and then I climbed out of the canyon."

"How could you tell that the—"

"Then," Siara continued pointedly, before I could finish my question, "I found a mass of demons collecting around a rather unremarkable piece of desert near the top of the canyon, and decided it was suspicious enough to be worth my attention. It would appear that I was right."

It would also appear that Siara's return had been the only reason that the Dragon reinforcements had finally come to our aid. She had tracked Aira down as soon as she was through the seam, then insisted that her dragons join the battle.

"General Aira has much to answer for," was all that Siara said about that particular infraction, after describing her arrival. I got the feeling she didn't want to talk about it in front of the non-dragon folk. That was fine with me.

"What do you wish to do with this?" Thanatos asked, as if anticipating the need for a change in subject, holding up the still-unconscious, balding mage that he'd routed out of MOME's forces.

That had seemed like a pretty significant tack away from the topic of demons amassing for an invasion to me, but everyone else let it slide, and I was too tired to bring it up myself. Besides, I was more pissed off at the MOME shitchip that Thanatos was holding than at Thanatos himself, so if he wanted to deflect, I was happy to let him.

"We need to interrogate him," Lizzie proclaimed. I hadn't seen the woman with olive skin (and I meant that literally, not as an unclear reference to Mediterranean heritage, but, like, actually the color of a green olive) enter the fray earlier, but I'd been distracted, and she was covered in enough blood and... dark goop that had probably come out of a demon, that I was fairly certain she'd been battling her heart out with the rest of us. "He can explain how they ripped open that seam, and how they made a deal with those demons in the first place!"

She sounded pretty angry for someone who helped run Unterberg, which was basically the Switzerland of the magical world and usually stayed so far outside of these types of conflicts that we'd had to essentially beg them to get involved in this one. Or rather, we'd tried and failed to beg them to help us. I thought they'd turned us down, but they were here now, and they'd definitely fought with us, so…

"I can speak to both those points, I'm afraid," said Thanatos.

It still startled me to see him in such a human guise, giant feathered wings notwithstanding. Granted, I'd only known him for an hour or so (less than that, if we only went by Earth time, instead of whatever weird timeline my life represented), but I'd seen him so often as an electric blue bunny or a giant clam/Cthulhu monster that the implacable angel look was definitely throwing me off.

"It is my understanding that the Ministry of Magical Entity officials had originally planned to inject an entity who possessed a surplus of dark matter with Technetium near the seam in La Paz, in order to attempt an invasion on Unterberg, the closest seam there being a relevant one. When that failed them, they tried to do the same thing on a smaller scale in Sucre. They succeeded, marginally. They managed to tear a small hole into one of the more frosty hell dimensions, or so my sub-ordinates reported at the time. Whatever they managed, they failed in finding a useful force for an invasion, and found nothing worth invading themselves. Our ice-dwelling brethren are often reluctant to leave their own world for any but the coldest regions of this one. They are… rather susceptible to any amount of warmth."

Those of us that weren't demons all exchanged looks. I, for one, wondered if Thanatos was really about to give us all the answers, and if so, why.

"Regardless," he continued, "they decided to try again, as I'm sure you're all aware. I was not truly cognizant of their intentions until word of their little attempted coup made its way even as far as my own realm." Thanatos turned his attention to me. "I did not lie to you when we first met, Vic. Their apparent plans for Technetium terrified my people. So, when a MOME representative offered my people freedom from such attacks in exchange for a small invasion—one which basically amount-ed to a free buffet lunch for my people—I accepted at once."

He took a deep breath, returning his attention to the whole group.

"However, MOME made it clear quite quickly today that they weren't planning to stick to their original offer. Rebecca Dryer—wearing someone else's skin—summoned me from my hell realm, even as my people marshaled for invasion. Then she injected me with Technetium, and only failed to destroy me, in the very way her people had vowed not to, thanks to the efforts of Vic, here. I believe I was summoned the second time in hopes that the Technetium would still be in my blood, but thankfully my metabolism is rather quick. However, I wasn't the only one summoned. As you all no doubt witnessed, another demon was summoned and injected. And we must all be grateful that the pour soul was rather starved, for they did far less damage that they might have—even less than a weak magical human would have, in all likelihood. The explosion must have been right on top of the seam when it happened, however, as it was sufficient to cause the rift MOME was hoping for. And… I believe you all know the rest."

"Why did you bother helping MOME at all, if Rebecca had already betrayed you once?" I asked, more than slightly baffled at Thanatos' casual explanation.

"It seemed her side was the winning one," he replied easily, as if it were just a simple truth and anyone else would have done the same. And maybe any other demon would have. I only knew one other, and it wasn't difficult to believe that Az might be an exception to the rule.

Thanatos smirked before continuing, "Although you quickly made it clear to me how wrong that assumption was. I corrected course accordingly."

I laughed. I had to. I mean, Thanatos was re-markably consistent in his self-preservation tactics, I had to give him that. And with so much evidence as to the duplicity of humans confronting him, I could hardly blame him for not holding out any loyalty to me, after I'd refrained from killing him gratuitously one time. That was a pretty low bar to pass, really.

"We will still need to confirm that story with Agent Elgby," Albert replied, gesturing to the un-conscious mage. "I'm sure you understand."

Thanatos nodded, not seeming the least bit offended.

"But where can we store him in the meantime? Not to mention all the injured MOME agents being pulled off the field right now," I asked. "It's not like we can trust that the MOME folks don't know a bunch of tricks for getting out of their own dungeons. Even if we could, it's not like we'll have locked them all up. And if any of them remain free, they could easily break the rest of their buddies out."

Albert and Lizzie nodded, though I noticed that Lizzie wasn't offering up storage options in Unter-berg. Thanatos said nothing. And Gwen. Damn it all, Gwen had left again.

I almost groaned in frustration. I had so many questions for her, I couldn't even tally them all up in my head. I wanted to find out where she had taken Trev, why she had showed up so many times without just fixing everything, since she was a freaking goddess anyway, and why she couldn't have warned me about any of the damned things I'd had to deal with lately, like, I don't know, turning into a dragon and then, more recently, a chimera.

And, oh boy, did I have questions about the chimera form. How was it even possible? Was that the whole reason that Sol, Seamus, and I had been thrown into this weird mating bond? Or could anyone do what we'd done? If it had been the reason for the mating bond, were we going to stop caring about each other, now that this whole thing was done? And that was just the tip of the iceberg. I had big plans for interrogating Gwen, hells yes, I did.

But all of that was going to have to wait.

"You could stow everyone from MOME in Hel's dimension, maybe. She owes me one, I think. Or maybe my parents could talk her into it. You should ask them, be—"

As if on cue, Gwen chose that moment to show up with both of my parents.

And I didn't know what to do or say to them, so I started backing away, so I wouldn't have to say anything at all. They could sort the rest of this stuff out. My parents knew more about the Hel realm than I ever would. It was possible they knew even more than Renata did, so, yeah. That just about ate up my reasons for needing to stick around this debriefing. They *really* didn't need my help.

But then my hand went to my forehead, as the thought of Renata reminded me that there was another group of people out there who really did.

NFORTUNATELY, MY BODY didn't seem to care that a hundred people were barely going to be able to take care of their most basic needs without me. I managed to reach for my Gwen-given powers and use them to transport myself to a familiar bit of abandoned desert in Northern Arizona, but as soon as I arrived my legs collapsed and my vision tunneled ominously.

A set of hands shrouded in mist caught me, before I hit the ground.

"Thanks," I muttered to Renata, while inwardly cursing the demons who'd tried to drain us at the end of the battle. I'd known I was weak, and second-guessed shifting my way out here instead of flying in dragon form, but I didn't see what choice I'd had. There was a whole group of people here who were going to literally be stumbling around the desert without me, and the longer I left them, the harder it would be to find them all.

So, here I was, and Renata's grip held me firm as I blinked the scrubby red desert and clear blue sky back into focus.

"I was hoping you'd be here," I said, trying to fill the silence while my body finished silently screaming at me to stop using my power.

Renata's voice was its normal sincere monotone.

"I assumed you had the battle under control."

I really couldn't tell if she was joking or not, but I laughed anyway.

The puzzled arch of her brows when I finally stopped, and stared at her, suggested she'd been serious.

"Did you not leave the battle victorious?" she asked.

I chuckled again, because I couldn't help it, then finally admitted, "Yes. Technically, I guess you could say that, but… I wish I had, at any point, felt even half as confident about my ability to pull that off as you seem to."

"You have many powers and many allies. There was little reason to think you would not succeed."

"Sure, except for the part where I have no idea what I'm doing, and where I was up against an entire army of mages and demons, and—never mind. You're right. We won, I guess, and I'm here now."

Renata smiled, as though I'd finally said something that made sense.

"Yes! Are you here to give me the whistle?" she asked.

I frowned.

"I hadn't planned to ditch you with over a hundred mind control victims," I said.

Finally looking at our immediate vicinity, after attempting to look into Renata's eyes through the continuously shifting mist that enveloped her started to give me a headache, I noticed that all of the aforementioned MOME victims seemed to be clustered nearby in various blobs of shade thrown by the occasional boulders. I also noticed that there were far more of them than we had initially dropped off here. Renata must have somehow wrangled the ones who had been on the opposing side back up here during the remainder of the fight…

"Did Gwen help you collect these folks?" I muttered, looking at the crowd huddled in the bits of shade they could find.

"It is noble of you to wish to continue to care for those you led from the dungeons," Renata said, ignoring my question about Gwen. "But how exactly were you planning to help? You can barely stand."

As if to prove her point, she released my arm, and my legs instantly rejected the idea of holding me upright any longer.

"Damn it," I mumbled, sparing myself from landing on my ass by kneeling with one hand on the ground to keep my balance.

I used the hand that wasn't keeping me from toppling face-first into a cactus to wrestle the whistle from my pocket, and shoved it in Renata's general direction. I felt it slip from my grip, but my eyesight had gone dark around the edges again.

"Is there a place that you would like me to take you, so that you may rest?" Renata's voice asked, from somewhere above me.

"Have you ever met a tree named Life?" I asked, shortly before passing out.

~~~

YOU REALLY SHOULD TAKE BETTER CARE OF YOURSELF, VIC.

I blinked a few times. The dappled light of the sun filtered through tree branches, softly warming my face, but also making it almost impossible for my vision to clear.
~~~

I sat up. I was delighted to find that I didn't pass out again, or even feel lightheaded.

YOU HAVE BEEN HERE FOR AN HOUR, NAPPING. YOU SHOULD BE IN FINE FORM NOW.

"Thanks, Life," I mumbled, even as I pulled myself to my feet.

I was wearing a pair of yoga pants, a well-worn sports bra, and a very soft T-shirt. For once, I was completely happy with the Gwen power's choice of clothes, although I didn't remember shifting forms at all, so I wasn't exactly sure why my clothes had shifted.

"Am I clear to use all my powers?" I asked, turning to see the glowing eyes sunk into the trunk of a tree that was shaped a little too much like the grim reaper for someone who went by the name of Life.

I WOULD NOT RECOMMEND USING THEM IN THE MANNER YOU HAVE BEEN, CONSIDERING HOW CLOSE YOU CAME TO BURNING YOURSELF OUT *AGAIN*, BUT YOU SHOULD BE FINE OTHERWISE.

"I'll do my best," I said, waving another thank you as I closed my eyes, thinking hard about the one place in the universe I really wanted to be.

O NLY TO BE hijacked by a red haired Goddess and snapped into the void.

I had been reaching for a specific destination this time, so winding up suspended in inky blackness with a red haired, green eyed, pale-skinned deity floating before me was more than a little disconcerting.

"What the actual fuck, Gwen?"

"What? I wanted to talk to you and I didn't want to keep your friends waiting."

"So, let me guess, you pulled us outside of time and space to have a chat?"

Gwen's smile made an almost glowing line across her face, and her emerald eyes glittered strangely, for being in a place that appeared to have no source of light.

"Yes! You're getting the hang of things now, aren't you?"

I laughed, though I almost felt like crying.

"You mean, now that we saved the world, am I finally getting a grip on how magic works? Yeah, I guess. Though I still have about a billion questions for you."

Her smile faded a bit, but she didn't disappear.

"Fire away," she said, her arms spread wide.

I cocked an eyebrow at her. This seemed suspiciously easy.

"Really? Ok… if you're really a goddess, why didn't you just swoop in and stop all of this from happening, instead of just randomly showing up to save our butts when it suited you?"

Gwen laughed, and spun in a circle that seemed to almost stir the inky blackness that surrounded us.

"A delightful question. Deities are willed into being by living things, not the other way around. As such, none of us are omnipotent, and we are all limited by the forms we are willed into. I am dark matter made into serendipity. My powers allow me to flit around any realm inhabited by earthlings, and help those who are already helping themselves. My powers won't allow me to directly affect any outcome."

My eyebrow rose again.

"Then how have you managed to save my ass, directly, on more than one occasion?"

Gwen clapped.

"Oh yes, that's a fun one. There are no written rules, per se, so I don't know exactly what we aren't allowed to do, but some of us seem to be permitted avatars, and we are allowed direct actions to save our avatars!"

"But the first time you saved my ass, I hadn't agreed to help you yet."

Gwen shrugged.

"The universe isn't as into consent as a lot of folks are these days. You were marked as my avatar the moment I decided to ask you. I waited to transfer my powers to you until you said yes, but the universe isn't as picky about that sort of thing."

Right. I supposed something older than time might not care about that sort of thing, if it cared about anything at all. As usual, Gwen's explanation was leaving me with way more questions than I'd started with, but at least she was answering me.

"Why did you send me on a quest to find out what happened to my parents, when what you actually wanted me to do was overthrow a magical authoritarian regime?" I asked, after a long pause.

That had Gwen cackling, for some reason.

"Oooh! This is so much fun," she squeed. "Why do you think?"

I just glared in response.

"Oh, come on, do you really want me to just tell you?"

I glared harder.

"Fine, fine. Sheesh. Way to take the joy out of it. If I had shown up and said, 'Hey, Vic, I need your help to take out an authoritarian regime that's making people's lives miserable, because I'm a deity that can't manipulate things directly,' would you have said yes?"

I wanted to just keep glaring, but instead I sat down on nothing, and crossed my legs while sighing profoundly.

"So you sent me on a personal quest that was almost guaranteed to help you get what you wanted, because it would put me in direct conflict with MOME?"

"YES! Oh, see, it is more fun to guess!"

If I could glare any harder, Gwen's hair would have been on fire.

"In the times that you showed up to help, sometimes you barely did anything. Sometimes you just made things harder, like when we had to haul your ass out of MOME's dungeons. What was up with that?"

Now Gwen just scoffed, and did a bit of her own glaring.

"Honestly, Vic, keep up. Outside of transportation, I generally can't affect things directly, unless it's down to saving just *your* ass. To make that battle go the way it needed to, you had to walk out those doors at *exactly* the right moment. The stakes were too high not to nudge you."

I thought about that for a moment, and was glad I was already sitting down in the void, so my legs couldn't give out on me.

"You mean, you... that... Dryer would have taken out the whole Earth if we had arrived earlier or later?"

Gwen nodded.

"The universe likes to remain intact. It pushed me very hard to go interfere with you. Luckily, Rhelia needed a ride anyway, and the dungeons suppress dark matter enough to make me a useless lump. Thanks for not leaving me there, by the way."

I sighed, rubbing my hands over my face and feeling like all the fight had left my body.

"I still don't get why you chose me, of all people, to help you out."

Gwen cocked her head to one side, raising an eyebrow at me.

"That's simple, Vic. You're one of the most naturally lucky humans I've ever met."

43

AND, AS I finally shifted myself to the place I'd been aiming for when Gwen hijacked me, I found it difficult to disagree.

It turned out that place was more of a person than anything else.

Or people, if you want to get technical.

A week ago, I was pretty certain that person had been Trev. A year ago, the people would have been my parents.

Instead, I found myself materializing in the middle of a cozy living room in the Andes, where Seamus and Sol were leaning casually, back to back, apparently laughing at something one of them had said.

The second I appeared, they both jumped to their feet, smiling and throwing their arms around me. I threw my arms right back around them. Sol's lips found mine first, and the kiss just about set fire to my skin, but we pulled apart after a moment, and when I turned to Seamus, I found a longing I couldn't name in his eyes.

"Are you always going to ask first?" I asked.

He nodded.

"My Moms really drove that lesson home," he said.

"Well, the answer is an enthusiastic yes," I replied.

And then Seamus' lips were lighting me on fire just as Sol's had, but with a bit more tenderness. Sol's affection was always a bit more assertive than Seamus' and… I found them both just as enticing.

When Seamus' kiss broke off, the three of us all still holding each other, part of me wanted to retreat to the bedroom with them, but a larger part of me just wanted to collapse on the couch and talk. Maybe have a couple of Sol's amazing sandwiches.

Judging by the fact that nobody stopped me from swinging my weight towards the couch, and the fact that they both collapsed with me when I did, I suspected the suggestion might be a popular one.

"Should I make us sandwiches?" I asked, honestly willing to make them, even though I was fairly certain I knew what the answer would be.

"Absolutely not," Sol replied, jumping up. "The thin abominations you call sandwiches are not allowed in my kitchen."

I laughed, though I didn't think my sandwich skills were that low.

"Fine," I agreed, starting to get up from the couch. "I'll make tea to go with the sandwiches."

Seamus leapt to his feet before I could get up, and pointed emphatically back at the couch.

"You will stay and rest. I can make tea. If Sol lets me."

He glanced sidelong at the kitchen, but Sol made no objection, so he headed into the small portion of the cabin that housed the teapot and tea collection, and then quickly returned to the "living room" in order to put the kettle he'd just filled on top of one of the burners that crowned the wood stove heating the whole place.

I sat on the couch and watched them both at work. I considered reading, but didn't think I'd be able to focus on printed words if I tried right now. Instead, I watched Sol sway expertly through her tiny kitchen, moving plates, bread, and sandwich fixings in a graceful dance. Periodically, I would glance at Seamus, who was also watching Sol, with a look I didn't quite understand in his eyes.

"Did you guys ever sort things out?" I asked. He had said something to that effect once, but I never really got the whole story. Not that it was entirely my business. We were all in a relationship, but that relationship was as open as it got. With the ground rules we'd laid out, none of us were beholden to each other for anything, really. Not now, at least. The relationship could change as we did, but we'd basically just decided that we were all too young and restless to offer each other more than sex and friendship. It was the friendship piece I was wondering about now.

I had intentionally asked the question loud enough for Sol to hear. I was asking both of them, although I'd directed the question mostly to Seamus. Sol had been… slow to warm up to the idea that he was a canine half the time.

"If you're asking if Sol apologized for being a bit of a bigot when we first met, the answer is yes."

I looked at Sol, who was smiling, and decided that was probably a good sign.

Probably.

"Why are you smiling like a bag of poop is about to drop on my head?" I asked, after a moment.

Sol actually cackled.

"Because I decided that to truly atone for my pigheadedness, I would introduce Seamus to my family as the man I was in a relationship with."

I could feel my eyes widen and I stared back and forth between them, wondering if I should laugh, or cuddle Seamus to protect him. The grin that went all the way to his eyes told me I needn't bother.

"And… why was that a good thing?" I asked.

Sol laughed again.

"My family, 100% werepanther for generations, according to Abuelita, considers themselves very progressive. No one batted an eyelash when I told everyone I was only interested in women. To be honest, I wasn't even worried about telling them, because I knew they wouldn't care. Tio Javi is married to Tio Rico, and Abuelita herself married a woman after she lost her husband in the war. But being involved with a wolf…"

I frowned.

"So how did that help?" I asked.

"Gatita, they *consider* themselves progressive. I led with the fact that I was in a poly relationship, and Abuelita just nodded like it was perfectly normal. Tia Rosa made one little huffing noise, but Primo Carlos actually applauded, and said 'That's only sensible in this day and age.' So how would they all look if they said anything negative when I introduced Seamus, and said he was one of the two people I was with? I could see Abuelita's face turn red, even as she smiled and welcomed him to the family. It. Was. Glorious."

This time Seamus laughed, and I finally felt the tension drain out of my shoulders. I was worried that Sol had put Seamus through an awful experience just to make a point, and maybe she had, but Seamus' eyes were glittering with mirth when he turned to me, so I didn't think so.

"Oh, don't worry, Vic, it was fine. Her folks are lovely. Her Abuelita was raining compliments on me by the time we finished dinner. Said I was a delightful young man."

"Did she add 'for a werewolf?'" I asked, with a barely restrained growl. People could compliment you all day and still insult both you and your heritage. It happened with damning frequency.

"Not once," Seamus said, looking earnest enough that I decided he wasn't just trying to placate me. "And I don't even believe she was thinking it, by the end. And even if she was, they've clearly been raised with a shitty mindset, and every single one of them was doing their best to just talk to me, actual me, and not their idea of what a 'werewolf' was."

"Like I said," Sol continued, "we consider ourselves progressive. Luckily, my family is actually progressive enough to admit to their own bullshit when they are called on it."

She paused for a moment, as she picked up a tray laden with some truly epic-looking sandwiches and brought them over to the coffee table that took up most of the space between all the couches and pillows.

"To be honest, I'm pretty damned ashamed that my family has believed that shit about wolves for so long, and that *I* believed it at all. I'm not sure who in my family had a falling out with a wolf at some point, but I sure as hell want to go back in time and slap them."

Then she looked up into my eyes and said, "Holy shit. Could we do that?"

And that had the three of us laughing uncontrollably as we dug into a feast of tea and sandwiches of historic proportions, and began a conversation about the myriad dangers and complications of time travel.

44

A FTER TWO MORE languid days of R&R with Sol and Seamus, I didn't really want to go visit my parents. Not only was I reluctant to leave Sol and Seamus—after all, those two days were the first time in our entire relationship when we'd had more than 24 hours without anyone trying to kill us, and it had been a wonderful haze of delicious sex, deep conversations, and ridiculous laughter. To me, the fact that were able to spend that long in a one-bedroom cabin without wanting to fight each other (quite the opposite, in fact) was proof positive to me that our relationship was about more than just the crazy three-way mating bond that had kicked things off.

Nothing about those two days made me want to leave the quiet coziness of Sol's cabin and the stark beauty of the Andes that surrounded it. Part of me was quite certain that I deserved much longer than three days of solace, after everything else that I'd been through.

But another part of me was worried that my parents were going to slip quietly back to Hel's realm before I could talk to them, despite Trev's reassurances via e-mail that Mom and Dad were planning to give me all the time that I needed before I spoke to them again.

That rankled too, to be honest—the idea that Trev was close enough to my parents that after ten years of abandonment and a few hours' worth of catching up, he could confidently proclaim to me that they'd still be there when I was ready to talk to them. Especially in place of them getting in touch themselves. As if Trev had some special insight into both their minds and mine? Even if he did, even if my parents were just respecting my boundaries by getting in touch via Trev…. The whole thing just felt contrived and stupid and… THAT was why I was shifting myself into Rhelia's home in the dragon realm, interrupting what looked like a perfectly boring round of Hearts.

"Vic!" Mom and Dad exclaimed together, dropping their cards in unison and standing up from the small, square folding table.

For a moment they looked like they were going to rush to me and embrace me, and then they stopped, at the last second.

I knew it was because they were worried it wouldn't be a welcome gesture, the rational part of my brain *knew* that, but it still hurt. The hesitation hurt, and maybe it was just a year's worth of pent-up grief and anger talking, but I lashed out.

"What, don't like the scars?" I asked.

It was an odd choice to bring them up; I'd rarely noticed the scars in the weeks since I'd gotten them. Sometimes they caught me off guard when I saw my reflection in passing, or when the skin on my shoulder felt tight when I pulled on a shirt, or did certain poses in yoga, and yeah, I was a little self-conscious about them when I was getting intimate with people—things that had really only come to my attention in the past few days, because honestly, my life had been way too much about running to survive another day and stopping the destruction of the known universe lately, and that didn't leave time for noticing well-healed scar tissue. So it was weird to use that as a barb against my parents, but it must have been a barb that caught, because their faces crumpled.

"How could you think that?" Dad asked, his voice a low whisper.

"Oh, I dunno," I said. "Maybe because you couldn't be bothered to come see my face in person after I risked my damned life *again* to save everyone, and was recovering in a remote mountain cabin."

Mom still looked hurt, but she'd regained her steel a little bit faster than Dad. "Trev told us you were healed, uninjured, that you just needed time to rest and spend time with your…friends."

"You mean my partners?" I asked, starting to feel anger on behalf of Sol and Seamus now. Hoping my parents were going to hand me an argument about being in a poly relationship instead of me taking everything else they said and using it against them. "The ones you haven't officially met yet, because you wouldn't come to visit? Those ones? Has being dead for a year set your thinking back twenty years, as well?"

It hurt to see Mom and Dad flinch with every accusation that passed my lips, but there was so much anger inside me in that moment that I felt like shifting to my dragon form and incinerating half the countryside.

"Vic, sweetie, what is this really about?" Mom said, as Dad just stood there and silently held her hand.

Oh good, at least they were in solidarity against me.

"What do you think it's about, *Mom*? You *left me.* You pretended to be dead to get away from me. You abandoned me for a year and left me alone to pick up the pieces. Do you have any idea what that was like for me? Do you? I was alone. With no one but Uncle Algy for a guardian, and an empty fucking house in Flagstaff as my inheritance. What did you expect when you decided to end the charade? A fucking party? Welcome home, Mom and Dad! We sure are glad you're back from your one-year vacation of not giving a shit about your child!?"

Mom and Dad just stood there, silently, their throats bobbing, but no noise escaping them, as I continued.

I noticed that Trev and Rhelia had discreetly abandoned the card table and they were standing quietly a few meters away. I couldn't blame them, really. I was fuming, and even letting all of this out didn't feel like it was helping—I was only getting angrier.

"Of course, I suppose I should be grateful that you only abandoned me for a year, shouldn't I? At least you didn't do to me what you did to Trev. Abandoning him to MOME for a decade!?

Forgetting he even existed!? Making *me* forget him!? My own brother? My twin? How could you?"

Tears were pouring down my cheeks and I was so far past caring that I didn't even swipe at them. I wasn't sure if they were from anger, or grief, or some horrible mix of the two—probably all of the above. I hadn't come here to yell at my parents. That really hadn't been the plan, but I was suddenly full of so much rage it felt like it was going to swallow me whole.

I didn't say anything else, because I wanted answers. None of the questions I'd posed had really been rhetorical, but Mom and Dad just stood there, gripping each other's hands like two people shipwrecked, afraid that their floating logs would be torn away from each other if they let go for even a second.

"How could you?" I repeated, since they didn't seem to understand that I wanted an answer. A real fucking answer.

When they remained silent, I turned and walked out the door.

TO MY SURPRISE, it was Rhelia who came to find me. I mean, I had reached for my dragon form and flown away the moment I'd cleared the door to Rhelia's house, so I guess I shouldn't have been too surprised. But Trev had wings too, and he was learning his way around the dragon realm, so I'd kind of expected him to show up.

Plus, you know, he's my twin.

"Your twin is unsssure of hissss welcome, at the moment, Living Cat," Rhelia said.

She was speaking with her human voice, probably because I had flown myself up to the cliff ledge that topped the dragon's prisons, then shifted back to human form in order to drape my legs over the edge and stare forlornly into the middle distance.

Somehow it just didn't seem appropriate to stare forlornly in dragon form.

I guessed she thought it was only polite that she talk to me in the form I'd taken. She stepped up beside me and gestured to the ledge to my right, as if asking for permission to join me. I nodded. She sat down.

Then we both just stared at the deep blue sky of the dragon realm, watching a few small wisps of cloud scuttle by. The drop beneath our feet was over a thousand meters, and the valley stretching out below us was unlike anything I'd seen on Earth. The grassy swath stretching out from the cliff was dotted with giant pillars of land that stood up like nails tacked into the green valley below. They were topped with tall grasses, just like the land behind me, but the pillars themselves were composed entirely of an almost yellow stone. Each pillar was the same height as the cliff that I sat upon, but while the ledge I was on stretched out to either side of me, running into the horizon, the pillars were just small islands of land, most of them no bigger than a small dragon, some as large as football fields, but all of them balancing precariously on single cylinders of stone. Hundreds of them dotted the valley that stretched a few kilometers in each direction, and ended on the other side with a cradle of low, sloping mountains that embraced the majority of the dragon city. I had no idea what lay beyond that view, but the whole thing was entrancing enough to keep me from thinking about anything else for a while.

It was Rhelia's voice that brought me back to the very thoughts I'd run away from.

"I am your family now, Vic, but I sssssensssse that I am not the persssson you wissssh to sssspeak with."

I chuckled.

"I like people I can just kick back and enjoy a view with."

Rhelia smiled, her yellow eyes glinting in the sunlight.

"I alsssso apprecsssssiate comfortable ssssssilencsssssessss with my companionssss."

Then she sighed.

"But I am concsssserned that sssssilencsssse issss not what you need, at the moment."

I sighed and lay back, my legs still dangling over the cliff ledge and my eyes gazing straight up at the sky.

"I don't want to yell anymore, Rhelia. I don't want to be this angry. It's... painful."

"Yessss, but will keeping it insssside you feel any better?"

I groaned.

"I take it back, you're no fun. I was really enjoying this bit of literal escapism. It's more direct than just reading a book at people, you know."

"Can you read a book *at* ssssomeone?"

"I don't know if *you* can, but I definitely can. It's a developed skill, really. Passive aggressively delicious."

Rhelia laughed, and hearing her laughter loosened a bit of the knot in my chest.

"Wanna call Trev over?" I asked, after a moment.

She nodded, but didn't move.

I wasn't sure why I didn't just call Trev myself. I could still feel him there, on the other side of our bond... but talking to him through it didn't feel right yet, somehow.

Maybe because I was actually furious with him.

Which was something I didn't realize until I sat up and saw him winging his way across the valley in phoenix form. He was beautiful, a giant, flaming bird of doom flying with the grace and ease of a lifelong predator. He may as well have been a bald eagle or a falcon. And yet, while part of me appreciated that beauty, and another part of me was relieved to see my brother on his way to my side, still a third part—currently a larger part than either of the other two—was filled with an almost incandescent rage at the sight of him.

He hovered in front of us for a moment, before swooping down to my left side and dropping into his human form exactly at the same time as he sat down beside me.

"Neat trick," I said, trying to find a smile for the twin I'd missed for more than half our lives.

"You don't look happy to see me," Trev said.

I guess my smile hadn't covered up the rage.

"I am. I'm happy that you're alive, and I'm happy that you're willing to talk to me again. I just… I'm really angry, Trev."

"And part of that is my fault."

It wasn't a question, so I didn't say anything.

The three of us stared into the distance for a while, as I searched for the right words for what I was feeling. It was particularly difficult because I was barely clear on why I was angry. For perhaps the first time, though, I was grateful to all the counselors I'd been forced to visit when Mom and Dad had "died."

"I don't think I'm actually angry with you—well, maybe a little bit, residually, for the whole knowing-about-Mom-and-Dad-being-alive-when-I-didn't thing—but mostly I'm angry *for* you. I'm angry for both of us. I know why they left you with

MOME. I understand that they thought they had no choice, but… I feel like they decided protecting me was more important than saving *you*, and I'm not sure I can ever forgive them for that. How could they, Trev? They made that choice for both of us! I know that's not the choice I would have made, if they'd asked. I would have told them not to worry about me, told them that the three of us should have broken you out and then gone on the run together. I've been evading MOME for months now, and I'm a freaking teenager! I'm sure we could have managed it as a family."

Trev reached out for my hand, and I gave it to him, our fingers lacing together in a reassuring knot.

"Are you mad at me for forgiving them?" Trev asked.

I considered that, for a moment.

"Maybe. I don't know. That's your choice, obviously. But… it's going to take me a long time to forgive them, Trev. I know they were trying their best, but damn it… if four teenagers can break into MOME and bust out everyone there, why couldn't *they*? Why did it all have to wait until we grew up and could do it ourselves?"

"Honestly, Vic, I am still amazed that we pulled that off, and it only worked because I knew how to hack into the system from the inside, and Sol had worked there, and even then we might have died if you hadn't had a friend who was a literal goddess… I'm not sure anyone else *could* have done it. And would you seriously recommend to a grieving set of parents, who had just lost one of their children, that they should risk the other child in a desperate attempt to save the one who was taken? I mean, they would have been risking losing *everything*. Leaving you in MOME's clutches, as well as me, and getting themselves locked up in prison, or worse. Missing both of our childhoods entirely."

I sighed.

"You've given this a lot of thought, haven't you?" I muttered.

Trev laughed, though the sound held little humor.

"I had ten years to think about it, didn't I?"

"Ten years that you could have spent learning to hate your parents," I whispered. "I'm sure MOME would have liked that."

Trev squeezed my hand again.

"I think MOME would have *loved* that. In fact, that's probably a big part of *why* I wound up forgiving Mom and Dad. MOME made every effort to turn the kids they'd taken against each other, and to turn us against our parents and families. They did everything they could to convince us that the people who loved us most hadn't cared enough to take care of us 'properly.' That we were a risk to everyone around us, and that if our families had truly loved us, they would have voluntarily handed us over to MOME for safekeeping. Lucky for me, they took me right around the time when I was starting to question adults. I didn't trust them from the start, and them telling me my family didn't take care of me properly? They couldn't have done anything to make me decide to forgive Mom and Dad faster. Once I was in my teens, it was like everything MOME did made me just want to come up with more reasons that Mom and Dad weren't to blame. MOME really should have invested in some child psychologists, if they'd wanted to succeed at turning us against our families. Instead, they had a bunch of guards and research scientists try to prod and bully us into it."

It was horrifying to think of, but also somewhat reassuring that MOME had been so bad at that particular job.

"So, yeah, I forgave Mom and Dad a while ago, and… look, I'm sure we'll have our differences yet. What family doesn't have their disagreements?

But, we have parents, Vic. Unlike so many of the people I knew growing up with MOME, we still have our family, and they still love us. Shit, they love us a lot. They haven't seen me in a decade, and I can *still* feel the love rolling off of them every time we hang out. They're pretty desperate to make things up to us."

I squeezed Trev's hand again and leaned back against the tall grass behind me. He and Rhelia did the same.

"I don't want to hate them. I don't hate them. I just… I grieved them for *a year*. The first few months… I was sure it wasn't true, that they weren't actually dead. The stories I made up in my head as to what had happened to them were almost as bizarre as what *actually* wound up being the truth. If they had shown up then, I think I could have shaken the whole thing off. I would just have been *relieved* that they weren't actually dead. Relieved my denial proved true. I would have been so damned grateful to have them back, grateful that the nightmare was just that, a nightmare, a farce, not reality. But that didn't happen. I eventually accepted that they were *dead*. I raged against it, I cried for hours, days, weeks, months, about it, but it was true. It had to be true, because they hadn't come back. I was certain they had loved me, and if they loved me and were still alive, they would have come back. When they didn't… it was finally, horribly true, and… it's not like I was over it, or anything, but I was growing into it as my new normal. Episodes of deep grief followed by mostly normal. Going whole days without thinking about them, or at least without feeling the searing pain of losing them. It was getting better. Tiny bits at a time, it was getting better. And *now* they're back. Now, *surprise*, they're not dead. And I'm glad they're not dead. Of course I am, but… they put me through that. They weren't really dead, but they put me through losing them. I know that they thought they were protecting me by leaving me behind, but they didn't even give me a choice. I'm not a child anymore, and they didn't give me a choice. I'm not sure I can forgive them for that."

Trev was silent for a moment before saying, "Makes sense to me."

I turned to look at him, his face so close to mine that I couldn't really focus on anything but his eyes.

"What? That's it?"

Trev stared back at me, but said nothing.

"You're not going to make their case for them? Tell me I'm being unreasonable?"

Trev smiled.

"First of all, emotions aren't reasonable, but they're natural, and there's nothing we can do about that. Second of all, I don't think you're being unreasonable at all. Your emotional response doesn't need to be grounded in reason to be valid, but, I mean… everything you just said is true, and if it were me, I'd be pissed at them too."

I just blinked at him for a moment.

"But *you've* forgiven them for far worse!"

Trev shrugged.

"I've had more time, for one thing. And for another, I'm not sure it was worse, Vic. Mom and Dad were trying to protect both of us as children, and that's what parents are supposed to do. MOME *stole* me. It's not like Mom and Dad just handed me over—they fought it as hard as they could, legally, but MOME threatened to take you, too, and it's kind of a miracle they didn't, really. It's not like they'd asked permission to take *me*… and then Mom and Dad, rightfully not trusting MOME to keep their word after they'd wiped all of your memories of me, disappeared, to keep you safe. They couldn't do that and try to bust me out at the same time. And honestly, if they'd been able to ask me, I would have told them to protect you too."

He must have seen the horror cross my face, because he frowned and continued, "Don't look at me like that. The whole reason that you're pissed at them on *my behalf* is because you feel the same way about it that I do. If given the choice of protecting your twin or yourself, you'd choose your twin. Right? You're angry because they chose to protect you over me, but if our situations had been reversed, I know you'd expect them to take care of me."

Ugh. He was so right that I didn't even say anything, I just turned to stare angrily at the sky.

"So, yeah," Trev continued, even though I wasn't looking at him anymore. "I get it. What Mom and Dad chose makes sense to me, and I have had years and years to process the whole thing. But what they did to you? You're right, they were protecting you by disappearing. And while you were still legally a child, they probably should have given you a choice, or at least given you some idea of what they were doing. I understand why they didn't, but I'm pretty sure it would piss me off if they'd done the same thing to me. I *know* it pisses me off that they did it to you. So, no, I don't think you're being unreasonable."

Rhelia hadn't said anything for a while, but she was still lying there, silent in her solidarity. And I found I took a surprising amount of comfort from her presence. She was starting to feel like a sister in more than just name. The three of us just lay there for a while, eyes to the sky, sun on our faces.

"So, what now?" I asked eventually.

"Musssst you forgive them in order to ssssspend time with them?" Rhelia asked quietly.

I considered the question.

"I suppose not, as long as they know how I actually feel."

"So, let's go tell them how you feel," Trev said, giving my hand another squeeze.

"And then?"

Trev chuckled.

"How about a game of Hearts?"

I toss the keys into the small bowl by the door and kick off my shoes before hanging my backpack from the coatrack. Then I reconsider, and put the bag containing over fifty pounds of textbooks on the floor, because the coatrack is solid, but it isn't invincible. The smell of fresh coffee pulls me down the hall into the brightly lit kitchen, and I wrap my arms around Seamus' waist as he distributes the pot evenly between three mugs.

"Is this ok?" I ask. The embrace is habitual now, but so's the question, and the answer isn't always yes. Usually, but not always.

"Quite," says Seamus, and he turns to hand me a mug of coffee.

I gesture at the two remaining mugs.

"Is Sol home yet?"

He shakes his head.

"Nope. We have a visitor."

I raise a questioning eyebrow.

"Check the living room," he replies.

I take my coffee mug with me.

Draped across the leather sofa that I'd bought to replace the one that had burned down with the rest of this house, over a year ago, is an ebon skinned, silver winged hottie who probably only looks male because I have just been hugging Seamus.

"Az!" I exclaim, placing my mug a little too hurriedly on the coffee table and jumping forward to embrace them.

"Hullo, Luv," they say, getting up and returning my hug with enthusiasm.

"You here for socializing, or research?" I ask, reluctantly letting them go and retrieving my coffee before settling myself into an adjacent IKEA chair.

"Can't it be both?" they ask.

"I suppose it has to, now I think about it," I reply, trying to keep the warm feeling creeping up my neck under control.

I am a big fan of the research that Az has been doing lately on behalf of the Council of Dark Matter Adjacent Peoples, or CODMAP, as I like to call it, much to Albert's annoyance. (Hey, it's better than MOME.)

And it is. Unlike MOME, which had been a regulatory body that was so corrupt it was essentially an authoritarian regime, CODMAP is a research and outreach program. It's doing its best to repair the centuries of damage that MOME has done to the magical (and non-magical) world, and it's trying to include as many previously silenced voices as possible.

"How are your studies going?" Az asks.

"They're interesting. I'm still hopeful that Earth biology will be a solid platform to start a xeno-logical studies branch once I graduate."

"Haven't your parents already started that branch?" Az asks.

"Nope. They're too singularly focused on dark matter to qualify. My current hope is to start cataloguing everything that lives in other realms, not just the things that interact with dark matter to function."

"Fascinating," Az replies, and the glint in their eyes makes me think that they're possibly just saying that because they're hoping to use me as a research subject again tonight. It's unnecessary. I'm always happy to participate in Az's research, anyway.

They are studying the various methods of in-gesting and modifying dark matter. It's related to my parents' research, but Az is in charge of their own sector, a fact I'm truly glad of, since I don't really want my parents having intimate knowledge of the experiments that Az and I are running.

Seamus comes into the living room with the remaining two mugs of coffee, and hands one to Az.

"Is tonight's experiment with all three of us?" he asks, sitting down on the far side of the couch from Az.

Az shrugs.

"If you'd like to see if we can bring on the chimera event again, that could be useful to the next phase of my—"

"Who didn't make me coffee just now?!" Sol's voice calls, as she enters the living room, carrying the now-empty coffee pot. "That's just cruel. Hi, Az. No chimera tonight. And Vic, we should probably reschedule our sparring. We have guests."

That has all of us looking interestedly behind Sol, and sure enough, my parents stand behind her, doing that awkward waiting-to-be-acknowledged-by-the-rest-of-the-group waddle that happens when you follow someone larger than life into a room.

I pop up to give Sol a kiss and go make some more coffee.

"Don't you have a gig tonight?" I ask, after a brief kiss.

"Not til 10," she replies, her arms lingering on my waist as I walk past her towards the kitchen. She's been playing enough bass gigs lately to completely cover her tuition for law school. I can't decide if I'm more turned on by Sol the musician, or Sol the future civil rights attorney.

Both. Why not both?

Reluctantly pulling away from Sol, I pause to give my parents a group hug on my way into the kitchen. Mom follows me.

"You don't have to cancel a chimera attempt just because we're here," she announces casually.

"Ugh, Mom, I appreciate you trying to be cool and all, but I am not having sex with Az with you and Dad in the house. Az is… not quiet, and the energy spill-over gets everyone going—that's how the last experiment wound up using all of us. If you want to find out what it's like to be in a house with a succubus doing a power exchange, you can invite Az over to your place sometime, and please never tell me about it."

Mom frowns, but I can tell from the muscles around her eyes that she's mildly relieved.

"I appreciate the support of my lifestyle choices, though," I add, half-jokingly. "Besides, Trev and

Rhelia said they would be staying over tonight, so that really just could not get any more awkward."

Mom says nothing, while I get the coffee brewing again.

I had initially been pretty reluctant to rebuild the house in Flagstaff. I hadn't been sure I wanted most of the memories that went with it, and besides, it had been too large for just me to begin with, and the plans my parents had for the rebuild had been ridiculous. Or they'd seemed that way until I figured out that Sol and Seamus were both happy to move in with me, as long as we each got our own room, and that Mom and Dad—who were still splitting their time between Hel's realm and their own rebuild of our Colorado home— were going to be visiting almost as often as Trev and Rhelia.

Turns out a five-bedroom is barely enough space, half the time.

Besides, funding the renos had made Uncle Algy feel quite a bit better after the whole holding-me-hostage-to-save-his-granddaughters thing.

"How long are you in town for?" I ask Mom, once the coffee is going. I can hear everyone else chatting in the living room, but I'm in no hurry to rejoin the group. Everyone in there is used to each other by now, and it's nice to just listen to the peaceful conversation as background noise.

"Not sure. Albert has a new theory he wants to test out, but he says he can't leave because it's finals week, and he'd have to put Ms. Rebuke in charge, and no one wants that."

She looks bemused, like she isn't entirely sure what that means, but is going along with it anyway, and I have to laugh.

"Probably true," I say, not bothering to explain about Rebuke—who has been decidedly… different after flying off with a succubus during a certain demon battle.

"How's school?" she asks, quietly, as if the topic is a prey animal she's afraid of frightening away.

"It's good, Mom. And you don't have to sound so careful when you ask about it. I am not studying biology just to please you and Dad. Asking me how things are going isn't going to influence me unduly."

Can you tell we've had this conversation before?

"I just don't want you to think that you have to—"

"She's fine, Mom," Trev's voice calls from the front door. It accompanies the sounds of boots stomping and fabric rustling around. "I would know if she weren't."

I laugh, and take the distraction of Trev and Rhelia's arrival as a chance to escape to the living room with the pot of coffee and a tray of mugs.

A few minutes later we are all settled into the living room, which should be huge, but now feels delightfully cramped.

Everyone has coffee or tea, depending on their preferences, and there are multiple threads of conversation going on throughout the room.

I feel warm, and happy, and realize with a tinge of surprise that *this* has become my new normal, somewhere over the past few months. We're still working to undo all the harm that MOME has done. It's a task so huge that we will probably never accomplish it, but we are making progress— after the first few months of total chaos—and things are starting to finally feel manageable. I'm not in danger of being killed every day. No one is asking me to save the world multiple times a week and… I'm doing what normal 19-year-olds do; going to school, having roommates, having romantic escapades with said roommates and the occasional non-roommate. You know, college stuff. And my relationship with my parents is almost normal as well. I no longer feel rage at what they did, just a sort of deep sadness that hits me sometimes. It's a sadness I can talk to either of them about when it comes up, and we've done a lot of hugging and crying together since they've come back.

Things are, dare I say it, good.

Trev clears his throat.

"Rhelia and I have an announcement," he says.

The whole room quiets and we all look at each other, equal parts puzzled and excited.

Rhelia stands up and points to her sweater, which contains a slight bulge.

My Dad starts to cry, and Mom clings to his arm, but then the bulge twitches and Rhelia hisses while reaching a hand underneath her sweater.

"We have desssscided to adopt a kitten!"

And she holds up the tiny feline like it is the greatest treasure on Earth.

Then we're all on our feet, laughing and cooing at the tiny black cat with bright green eyes, as it stares bewilderedly at far too many big things crowding around it.

Almost at the same time, Sol and I shift to our cat forms and plop down on the ground in front of it. Rhelia sets it between us and it mews and squeaks, in the way that only kittens can. Sol gives it a lick, and I stick my nose out to give it a welcoming sniff.

Then it boops its tiny pink nose to mine, and everything is perfect.

This concludes Vic's adventures… for now.

If you'd like to collect all five books in one place be sure to check out: *Victoria Marmot the Complete Collection*

Other works by Virginia McClain

The Chronicles of Gensokai Series:
Blade's Edge
Traitor's Hope

Short stories:
Rain on a Summer's Afternoon

Follow Virginia on social media:
www.virginiamcclain.com
twitter.com/gwendamned
facebook.com/virginiamcclainauthor

Acknowledgements

These books wouldn't have been possible without a fair bit of help from a number of people. My deepest gratitude goes out to the following people:

My editor, Aurora Wilson-McClain, for not only working with my sometimes ridiculous deadlines, but also for helping me sort out the best use of obscure spell references, the number of "s"s a certain dragon uses in her speech patterns, and where, exactly, everyone has left their clothes.

My husband, for putting up with me disappearing every evening for months on end in order to get these books written, for being my best cheerleader and for not giving me too much grief when I failed to get my half of the housework done.

Cedar, for letting me ignore her often enough to get formatting done, as well as promotion and marketing stuff, and for being so willing to hang out with her wonderful caregivers.

Anne, Lee, Jim, and Gabi, for keeping Cedar entertained, fed, and happy so that I could write.

To my proofreaders: Corey & Paul.

To my Patreon supporters: Paul, Corey, Mishy, Marie, and Jessica.

And finally, the folks at Stella's au CCFM for always putting up with me occupying a table for hours on end while only ordering a cup of tea.

Virginia McClain is an author who masqueraded as a language teacher for a decade or so. When she's not reading or writing she can generally be found playing outside with her four-legged adventure buddy and the tiny human she helped to build from scratch. She enjoys climbing to the tops of tall rocks, running through deserts, mountains, and woodlands, and carrying a foldable home on her back whenever she gets a chance. She's also fond of word games, and writing descriptions of herself that are needlessly vague.

For more information check out
www.virginiamcclain.com
facebook.com/virginiamcclainauthor
twitter.com/gwendamned
bookbub.com/author/virginia-mcclain

9 781999 461225